IF YOU'RE READING THIS...

KIERSTEN MODGLIN

KIERSTEN
MODGLIN

Cover Design by Kiersten Modglin
Copy Editing by Three Owls Editing
Proofreading by My Brother's Editor
Formatting by Kiersten Modglin

First Print and Electronic Edition: 2022
kierstenmodglinauthor.com

*To Sara, both Erins, June, Dee, Heather, and Aunt Rhonda
—for every wild adventure we've had and for all the
adventures yet to come. Cool.*

PROLOGUE

I was the kind of thing people would write songs about.

A walking, talking commercial.

Something families would discuss over Sunday dinners or during drives to softball games.

Did you hear?

How terrible...

A bride on her wedding day—still dressed in white, though it was tattered, torn, and bloody now—sitting in the waiting room of our local emergency room, mascara staining both cheeks, waiting for the doctors to confirm what I'd prayed for hours wouldn't be true.

But as the hours ticked on, as the time passed, I felt it in my gut. He wasn't coming back to me.

When a doctor walked out of the double doors with a solemn expression, pulling his mask from his face with a limp hand, I knew.

I'd been through this before—the metallic smell of

blood mixing with the strong, bleached scent of the waiting room, the nervous pacing of families and loved ones all around, my heart racing against the blips and beeps of the machines in nearby rooms, the sound of gurneys being rolled down hallways, of doctors speaking in hushed tones.

It was old hat by now.

A sick, ironic joke no one but the universe seemed to be in on.

He was gone.

Phil was gone.

I felt hands on my back before the doctor made it to us.

James.

Eric.

Jerry.

I wasn't alone, and yet, I was. I was completely and utterly alone.

Across the room, his mother's heart-wrenching wails filled my ears, drowning out the sounds of the doctor's apology. His explanation.

They'd done all they could do.

There was nothing else.

He was gone.

The love of my life; my Phil. He was gone.

It was supposed to be the happiest day of our lives.

The beginning of the rest of our lives.

Now, everything we'd planned was torn to shreds. And I had no idea why.

In a split second, everything had changed. Everything

had been ruined. Ripped away from me when it was all so close.

With a cruel twist of fate, what should have been *lives* became *life*.

Two became *one*.

We became *just me*.

Mrs. became *Miss*.

You thought you could find happiness...

Don't you know better by now?

It wasn't supposed to go this way.

CHAPTER ONE

ONE YEAR LATER

They say the first year is always the hardest—but I never got to find out.

That was what I was thinking about as I packed my bags for the first-anniversary trip my husband would never get to go on. As I folded my clothing carefully into the luggage we received as a wedding gift from my stepfather—matching luggage for the many trips we'd someday take.

Now, his suitcase sat in the corner, a constant reminder that he'd never take another trip with me. That we'd never once get to take any of the trips we'd dreamed of. A sunset stroll in Hawaii, a romantic getaway to Santorini, a penthouse apartment with a perfect view of the Eiffel Tower in France, hitting the slopes in Switzerland. As quickly as you could snap two fingers—all our plans had vanished.

I'd give anything to have gotten through the hard days they warn you about. The screaming fights. The nights with one of us sleeping on the sofa. As if nothing could be worse than that.

Some people might say I'm lucky—in fact, some rather rude people have said just that. That my memories with Phil will always be happy. That we loved each other until the last moment and I'll never have to live with regret over harsh words spoken or wounds that would never heal.

Of course, our relationship wasn't all roses. We had our share of fights, like everyone does, but I loved him.

As much as one can love another human being.

And he loved me, too.

I closed the luggage, zipping it up just as the sound of the doorbell chimed through the house. Taking a deep breath, I moved across the room and then across the house.

I was still fighting back tears as I swung open the door and took in the sight of James, standing there waiting for me. His warm, caramel skin, perfectly faded hair, and chiseled jaw.

"It was locked."

His smile warmed me, taking me back to the lazy afternoons spent under the oak tree in my backyard as a child. Afternoons playing make-believe and dreaming about what the future would look like.

If only we'd known...

Spying the pain that must've been etched into my face, he pulled me into a one-armed hug, the crisp, clean scent of his soap hitting me. I closed my eyes, hugging him tighter.

"We're going to get through this," he promised, pulling out of our hug too quickly and looking me over. His jaw twitched. "You aren't alone. Not now, not ever."

I nodded. "Thank you for coming with me."

He pursed his lips. "Are you kidding? You know I wasn't going to miss this."

I couldn't fight my smirk as I tilted my head toward the kitchen. "Do you want anything to drink? I'm just getting the rest of my things together."

"Nah, I've got a coffee in the car. Need help with anything?"

"Actually, yes. Want to help me lug the suitcase so I can get the rest of my stuff?"

"Sure thing. Where's everyone else?"

We made our way toward my bedroom and, once there, he pulled my suitcase from the bed.

"I haven't heard from Miles, but Eric should be here any minute."

I didn't miss the way he rolled his eyes at the mention of Miles. Last time the four of us were together, they hadn't exactly gotten along. I could never quite get a read on the two of them. One minute, everything was fine. The next, it was one snide remark after the other.

I'd learned to ignore it.

"Can you help me with this?" I asked, reaching for the white cardboard box at the top of my closet.

"You got it." He jogged around the side of the bed, squeezing beside me, and grabbed it from the top shelf. He passed it to me after peering inside. "Are those from the wedding?"

"Mm-hmm." I wrapped my arms around it, hugging it close to my chest as I recalled the afternoon Phil and I had spent trying to put the box together. Folding this piece and tucking that one. It had been enough to give us both headaches as it collapsed for the fourth time.

I fought against the tears burning my eyes again, looking down.

"You haven't opened them yet?"

A longing sensation filled my chest, so intense it was painful, and I swallowed. "I couldn't. They're meant to be opened on our first anniversary."

"Well, yeah, but..."

But you didn't make it to your first anniversary. He's dead.

The truth of it hung in the air between us, unspoken yet there.

"I just couldn't do it. I'm...I'm not even sure I'm ready to do it now. But I have to."

He put a hand on my arm. "You don't have to do anythin—"

The sound of my phone ringing interrupted us, and I reached for it on the nightstand.

"Sorry, just a sec."

"Is that them?"

I sighed, spying the name on the screen. "It's Amber."

He didn't bother trying to hide his scowl. "What does she want?"

I shrugged one shoulder as I pressed the phone to my ear. "Hello?"

"I can't."

I paused, processing what she'd said. "Amber?"

"Yeah, who else?"

"You can't what? I'm confused."

"Uh, did you not text me and ask if I could check on Jerry this weekend?"

Realization clicked in for me. "Um, yes. Two days ago. He's just not been feeling well. I've been taking him soup and I just refilled his prescription, so you literally just need to call and make sure he's taken them every day around ten and two. And then I usually call at night, but sometimes he's sleeping and—"

"I can't," she repeated, cutting me off. "I've got plans."

I pinched the bridge of my nose. "It's just a few phone calls to make sure he's okay. I would do it myself but this weekend is—"

"I'm sorry. I can't. I'll try and text him if I get a chance, but no promises. You're better with that sort of thing anyway."

"That's what I'm trying to tell you… I've been doing it, but I'm going away this weekend for the wedding anniversary. I'm not sure what I'll be doing or how much service I'll have, so I really need you to handle this for a few days. Just make sure he doesn't need anything."

She sighed. "It's just a cold, isn't it? Why do I have to check on him?"

"You know what? It's fine." I waved a hand in the air. "I don't have time for this. I'll just take care of it."

"Thanks. You're the best." She sent an air kiss through the phone and ended the call.

I threw the phone down with a huff.

"Jerry's sick?"

I'd nearly forgotten James was still there as I massaged my temples. "He's got bronchitis, but he keeps forgetting to take his medicine. I was trying to see if Amber would help me out this weekend, but—"

"Let me guess, she's busy."

"Bingo." My smile was small and bitter when I met his eyes.

He stepped forward, brushing a hand across my shoulder. "I'll help remind you to call and check on him. We'll make sure he's okay."

I rested my head on his chest, puffing out a breath. "What would I do without you?"

"Be lost, obviously."

I chuckled just as someone opened the door in the living room, and he pulled away. "I'll go see who it is."

I nodded, unable to speak as I attempted to pull myself together. Elephant in the room: my three closest friends were men. It was odd to a lot of people. James had always been my best friend, but before Phil's death, I had several other friends, too. After his death, it became too hard. Too hard to see the ones who were in happy relationships. Too hard when they pressured me to talk about my feelings. Too hard to have the conversations they wanted to have.

Miles, James, and Eric were the exceptions to all of that. With them, we talked about everything *except* our feelings. They made me laugh. They didn't treat me like I was made of glass; didn't act as if being a widow was the biggest part of my personality. They didn't stare at me with those looks I got from others—full of pity and heartbreak. Didn't say things like *I can't even imagine* or *he's in a better place.* They just let me breathe. Let me laugh and talk about whatever I wanted to—or nothing at all, for that matter. They let me feel like I was normal. Like my life was normal. I needed that. I needed to be surrounded by people who would let me forget, if even for a second. It really was as simple as that.

Moments later, James returned with Eric just behind him. His dark-brown hair was perfectly styled as usual, his cheeks and chin boasting a good bit of stubble that meant he hadn't shaved in a few days.

"Hey." His gaze lingered on mine for a second too long, as if trying to gauge how upset I was, and then he looked away, shoving his hands in his pockets with a breathy sigh. "You about ready?"

"Just about." If there was anyone this weekend would be hard for, aside from me, it was Eric. In truth, I was just as worried about him as I was myself.

By now, though, we were masters of pain. Well practiced in the art of breathing through it and pushing forward.

Here goes nothing…

He gave a thin-lipped smile. "Anything I can help with?"

"I don't think so. We're just waiting on Miles." I glanced at the clock, realizing he was nearly half an hour late, and picked up my phone. "I'd better try to call him."

Eric and James exchanged a knowing glance.

"While you're at it, we'll load up the car. Is this it?" James gestured to the suitcase on the floor next to him and the lone toiletry bag left on the bed.

I nodded, searching for Miles's phone number in my contacts before pressing the phone to my ear as Eric lifted my bag from the bed then followed James and my rolling luggage out the door.

"Almost there." When Miles answered, he was calm and cool—his voice like pure butter as it trailed into my ear. I don't think I'd ever heard him be anything but absolutely sure of himself.

"You're late." My fingers caressed the delicate detailing of the cardboard box in my arms.

"Ah, better late than never, as they say." I heard the car shut off, alerting me that he'd arrived. Finally. "I'll be at your door in two seconds."

"Well, don't bother. Just meet us at the car. We're on our way out."

"Whose car are we taking... Never mind. I see them. *'Sup?*" His voice was loud through the speaker, though it sounded like he'd leaned away from it.

Without saying goodbye, I ended the call and crossed my bedroom.

Mine.

Just mine.

Though it should've been ours.

I flicked off the light and closed the door, hugging the box closer to my chest as I thought of him.

I wish you were here, babe.

I wish you were with me.

Outside, the boys had already loaded the bags into the trunk of Eric's silver Mercedes when I arrived. I tucked my keys into my faded-green handbag as I approached them.

"Ready?"

At the sound of my voice, all eyes fell on me.

"Whenever you are." Miles tucked a piece of his dark, shoulder-length locks behind an ear, and I caught a glimpse of what looked like a new tattoo on his arm. He was running out of space for them.

"Want me to put that back here?" James eyed the box in my hands, and I pulled it back with a knee-jerk reaction that was completely unnecessary.

"I've got it."

He reached for the car door, pulling it open. "Who's riding where?"

"I'm driving." Eric already had his keys out as he reached for his own door and slid inside.

"I call shotgun." Miles made no actual moves to stake his claim, instead watching me closely as if to see what I'd do. Then, proving me right, he added, "That okay?"

"Sure. I'll ride in the back with James." I slid into the back seat and placed the box to my left, keeping it safe there as if it were Phil himself.

The box of letters was personal. Private. But I couldn't open it alone.

I knew what it would do to me. I knew how badly it was going to hurt. Still, I had to do it. I knew James thought it was silly, or self-destructive, and it probably was. I couldn't explain why I needed to put myself through it—not to them, or to myself—but I had to.

"Alright, Blondie, you get to pick the music this time." Eric passed me his phone, catching my eye in the rearview with a wink.

"But...it's James's turn." I started to hand it to him, but he pushed it back to me.

"It's fine. We decided. This is your weekend; you should be the one to choose." Eric offered me a small smile, and I felt myself starting to tear up. It was the simplest gesture, really, but I was already a ball of emotions that weekend, so I suspected it wouldn't take much at all to have me crying.

Trying to hide my tears again, I turned my attention to the phone as Eric backed down the short driveway, now lined with extra cars, and into the street.

I selected something fun, a Taylor Swift album—a new one Phil would've loved—and the playful groans were instantaneous.

"Can I change my vote?" Miles quipped.

I reached up to the front seat and swatted his arm, placing the phone in Eric's outstretched hand. "No complaining on this trip," I chided them all. "Hear me?"

"Whatever you say." Miles leaned back against the headrest, adjusting the round-lens sunglasses on his nose as Eric turned the music up louder, and we were off.

I'd been planning this weekend for a long time—a celebration of what should've been. A way to say goodbye to the life and the love I should've had.

Happy anniversary, babe. Miss you.

CHAPTER TWO

The vacation rental wasn't too far from home, so it was just two hours, including traffic, before we arrived. The house was small and yellow with a steep driveway leading down to a garage.

"Where's the pool?" Eric almost sounded disappointed at not seeing it immediately.

"It looked like it was down a hill in the pictures, so I'd bet it's right over that balcony." As the car came to a stop, I stepped out of it, breathing in the humid air. The sun reflected off the light-blue deck just in front of us, matching the steep staircase that led to the house.

James moved past me, taking the steps two at a time to stand on the balcony and look down. "Jesus..."

"Nice?" Eric rushed over to join him. Together, they were like two puppy dogs. Or children. Overly excited over life's simplest things.

Then again, I'd learned it was better to be overly

excited than not excited at all. I wished I could go back and appreciate the moments I'd had with Phil more.

That I'd put down my phone more often.

Laughed when he told me a joke, even if I was in a bad mood.

That I'd done everything I could, every moment of the day, to make sure he knew how appreciated and loved he was.

"It's huge," James called over his shoulder. "Even bigger than the pictures made it seem."

"Check out the firepit." Eric gestured to the chairs gathered around the rusty black bin. "Did anyone think to bring wood?"

"There's a wood stack and an axe over here." Miles was leaning over the gate, peering into the backyard.

"Should be everything we need, according to the listing. Let's get the bags inside and we'll figure out if we need to make a store run for anything."

Seeming to remember there was still work to be done, James spun around and jogged toward me. Eric took a final look at the pool, then pulled out his phone to snap a picture. Miles moved slowly back to me, twirling a stick between his fingers.

"It's so quiet out here." Eric lifted a hand to his brow, shielding his eyes from the sun as he slowly took in our surroundings.

"I know. It's hard to believe so close to the city, isn't it?" I rested my hands on my hips, sucking in a breath of fresh air.

"Probably the trees." He slid his phone back out of

his pocket, holding it up to examine the screen as the wrinkle in his forehead deepened. "Hopefully we still have enough service to get calls." He lowered his eyes to meet mine. "You said there's Wi-Fi here, right?"

"Yes, but *you* are not supposed to be working on this trip." My tone was pointed as I passed his suitcase to him. "Remember?"

"I know. I'm not. I'm just waiting to hear back from one client about an offer we're putting in. I told everyone else I was out of town." He sighed. "This was already supposed to be done, but they're taking their sweet time about making a decision. It'll be a wonder if the house doesn't go before I hear from them."

Miles let out a loud snore from where he stood at the front of the car, resting his head against the bright-silver roof.

"Oh, fuck off." Eric shoved him with his suitcase, causing everyone to burst out into laughter. At least everyone was getting along. For the moment, anyway.

"Sorry, I just dozed off there. Go on, though. Really, it's riveting." He leaned forward, grabbing his bag and one of mine.

"Well, we can't all play rock stars all day, can we?" Eric shoved past him, reaching for his own bag.

"Play nice, boys," I warned.

"Yes, Mom," came their immediate responses as they turned to walk away, identical sly grins adorning their lips. James and I grabbed the last of the luggage, and I stopped briefly to pull the box from the back seat before we made our way up the stairs.

"What's the code?" Eric gripped the keypad, swiping sweat from his brow.

"I'm looking..." Miles scrolled through his phone in search of the answer.

"Twenty-twenty." I didn't need to look it up, the number burned in my mind like it did for so many people now.

Eric tapped the number in and twisted the knob. The men stepped back, allowing me inside first.

The home was small and quaint—cottage-like. In the small kitchen, my eyes danced over the wooden cabinets, the wire basket of a variety of teas, the bee-shaped napkin holders on the table, and the various plants hanging near every window.

Eric jogged ahead of us across the living room and toward the stairs as James shut the door. "Three bedrooms, and there are two beds in each room. How are we doing this?"

Miles stopped at the bottom of the stairs as Eric's question echoed through the house. He stared at me, waiting for me to decide.

"Colbie should get to pick her bed first," James said, nudging me gently.

"Oh, I don't really care." Truth was, I hardly slept anymore anyway. I would spend most of the trip downstairs in front of the television—the only thing that seemed to allow me to escape my reality these days.

"He's right. You should pick." Miles patted the handrail as Eric reappeared, making his way down the stairs.

"Well, what'll it be, m'lady?" He gestured up the stairs as we began to follow him.

The top floor landing had three rooms, just as he'd said. One to the right, one to the left, and one straight ahead. Upon further examination, the rooms all looked nearly identical. Two full-size beds, a smaller-than-was-ideal television, and a closetful of extra bedding in every bedroom. They each had a small station with a single-pot coffee maker and snacks.

The differences seemed insignificant—one room had a small metal desk, another had a mini-fridge, and the third had a window seat.

"It doesn't matter, guys," I told them, after checking out each of the rooms. "I don't plan to spend a lot of time in any of the rooms. I just need a place to crash. Do you all have preferences?"

"The desk would be useful in case I need to do some work." Eric gestured toward the laptop bag at his feet.

"And I could use the mini-fridge to store my insulin," James said, "but it's not a big deal. I can use the fridge downstairs."

"No, that's fine. Miles, that leaves you with the room with the window seat. That work?"

"Maybe you'll write us a song," Eric teased.

"Yep. Fine. Whatever." Miles lugged his bag over his shoulder, cutting a sharp glance at Eric. His eyes fell back to me. "But you still haven't answered the question about where you'll be sleeping."

"Oh, right. Well, um, it doesn't matter. I can just crash on the couch if I need t—"

19

"No way."

The response from all three men was instantaneous. "You aren't sleeping on the *couch*." Eric grimaced as if I'd said I'd just sleep outside. "This is your trip. I'll sleep on the couch. I can work at the table."

"No one needs to sleep on the couch. There are plenty of beds." Miles lowered his bag again. "Just decide who you're rooming with. What's the big deal? What, do you wanna draw straws?"

"You can stay with me," James offered, jutting his head toward his bedroom door.

"Or me." Eric patted the doorframe. "My room has the most space."

I looked between them, two sets of hopeful eyes. This trip was about me, and I knew they all wanted to make me comfortable, but I hated being forced to choose between them.

"How about this? There are three rooms and we're staying three nights." Miles heaved his bag and guitar case through the crowd, disappearing into the room and placing them down with a loud sigh. "Why don't you just room with each of us for one night? That way you don't have to pick favorites."

That's essentially what I was being asked to do, wasn't it? Pick favorites. And how could I ever do that?

James was the friend I'd known the longest—the one who'd made mud pies with me and ran in the sprinkler when we were five, the one who played in the tree house and made prank calls when we were twelve, and the one who stressed about finals and prom dates with me when we were teens.

Eric had been Phil's best friend, but since his death, we'd both taken up that space in each other's lives. We'd fallen into a rhythm. When I needed new tires, it was Eric I went to for advice. When he needed someone to get a beer with and watch the game, he came over or invited me out. In some strange way, I felt closest to him, maybe closer than James even, because we shared the same wound. Our grief recognized something in each other. The Phil-shaped hole in our lives couldn't be explained to anyone else.

And Miles... Miles was hard to explain. He was the person I knew the least, but he'd been there with me after Phil's death in a way no one else could. At the time, he was nothing more to me than our wedding singer. We'd spoken a handful of sentences to each other at most. When he'd come by to deliver flowers days before the funeral—planning to leave them on the doorstep—he'd found me sobbing on the porch of our home instead.

Any normal person would've walked away or made an excuse to leave, and I wouldn't have blamed them. But Miles, he'd just sat down next to me and held my hand. He didn't say a word, just stayed with me as long as I needed. Comforting me wasn't his responsibility, but he didn't seem to realize or care about that.

He'd been the shoulder I leaned on, the one person I could completely fall apart in front of—even more so than Eric—because I didn't have to be strong for him.

Every time I thought about them, I couldn't help

comparing the men. Though they were typically civil with each other—sometimes bordering on friendship—and had spent the last year together nearly once a week at a minimum, it didn't change the fact that each of our friendships was different and I was the connecting factor.

I was the glue, and if I began to choose a side, began to pull away from two to be closer to one, all of this—my entire support system—fell apart.

Realizing everyone was still waiting on me to make a decision, I nodded. "That sounds good. I'll room with James tonight, Miles tomorrow, and Eric on Sunday."

"Awesome." James lifted his bag, stepping into the room just ahead of us and checking over his shoulder as we all fanned out. "This room's pretty nice, hmm?"

"It's really nice, yeah. This whole place is beautiful."

"Which bed do you want?"

"Well, I'm just here for the night and you're here for three nights, so why don't you pick? This bed has the best view of the TV, but this one's closest to the refrigerator. Which is more important to you?"

"You know me. I'm not picky." He shrugged. "I'll probably read before bed anyway. There's never anything on." He was still lingering, waiting for me to decide and being too accommodating when I knew the TV helped him fall asleep most nights.

"Okay, well I'll let you have the bed in front of the TV, just in case." I moved past him toward the bed on the far side of the room and dropped my suitcase on top of it.

As he was retrieving his bag of insulin, there came a

knock on the door and Miles appeared in the open doorway, already dressed in his swimming trunks.

"Hurry up, slowpokes. We're going down."

"Be right there." I grabbed my own bathing suit as he dashed away.

"Should we order dinner first? Or make a grocery run?" James asked, still unpacking.

"Let's order delivery." I tucked a stray blonde curl behind my ear. "Pizza sound good?"

He already had his phone out as I crossed the room, breathing out a sigh. I'd worried about what this weekend would hold. Once, I'd pictured our first anniversary laden with chocolate-covered strawberries, champagne, and dinner near the ocean. Never once did I expect I'd be spending it with three men who weren't my husband. Never once did I imagine Phil wouldn't be there at all.

But I could do this.

If I could make it through the weekend, like I'd made it through this last year, I could make it through anything.

Wish you were here...

CHAPTER THREE

We stank of chlorine, bug spray, and sweat that evening, still wrapped in our beach towels at the wrought iron table on the top deck.

Miles tipped his beer back in his mouth as Eric tore the paper label off of his. Next to me, James was lighting the citronella candle in the center of the table.

The box of letters sat directly in front of me.

Taunting me.

Reminding me of why we were here.

That I was actually going to have to do this alone.

"You don't have to do this, you know?" As if he'd read my mind, Eric met my eyes across the table. "You can wait until you're ready. Or not read them at all. It doesn't matter."

"He's right." James placed the lighter down. "He wouldn't have wanted this. Phil wanted you to be happy... This is only going to bring you pain."

"Maybe." Miles leaned forward, resting his elbows on

the table. "Or maybe it'll bring her peace… Comfort. The people who wrote those letters care about you." He met my eyes next. "They're here for you. Maybe that will help you, but only you can know that."

"She doesn't need the letters to tell her who's there for her." James put a protective hand over my arm. "Who's always been here for her."

Miles shrugged one shoulder, taking another sip of his beer. "Doesn't mean it's not nice to hear it occasionally. At the end of the day, *you* have to decide, Colbie. Only you."

"I want to open them." I pressed my lips together, sounding more confident than I felt before looking at Eric, then James. "I know it's going to be hard, but I feel like I have to do it. For Phil, but also for me."

"We're right here." James squeezed my arm gently before releasing it and sliding away.

"You don't have to be." I shot a glance at Eric, speaking only to him. "I know this'll be just as hard on you."

He nodded, looking apprehensive. "You know I'm not going anywhere. Phil would've killed me if I weren't here for you."

I reached for the box, a sudden tightness in my chest as my fingers connected with the rigid cardboard. I pulled it toward me, lifting the lid.

The smell of the wedding came back to me—the sugar of the buttercream icing, the cleaner they'd used to mop the floors, the dust from the room where the chairs had been stored, the cologne Phil had worn. It was all there, clinging to the silky-smooth paper of the letters, the glue of the envelopes.

Tears fell without warning and I blinked them away, focusing on the task at hand.

The men sat silently, letting me work through my grief before I reached for the first envelope. If they were uncomfortable, there were no signs of it.

By now, they'd seen me cry more times than I could count.

Retrieving the envelope from the top of the jumbled stack, I read over the scrawled handwriting.

Mr. and Mrs. Tanner

I bit my tongue, swiping my nail under the corner of the envelope and tearing it open.

Well, you made it to a year and neither of you killed each other...congratulations!

Tears blurred my vision, making it impossible to read what was in front of me. I blinked, allowing them to fall.

I know the first year is hard, kids, but I'm so proud of you both. Your uncle Jim and I love you so much. My advice: always listen to each other. Always kiss good night. Never go to bed mad. Remember that you're one team—there's no winner or loser unless you both win. If you ever need advice, Lord knows I'm full of more. But I just wanted to say how excited I am to see what the future holds for you two.

Oh, and give your auntie some babies to snuggle soon, Phil. I won't live forever.

Love you kids,

Aunt Jean

PS Colbie, honey, you looked beautiful today. Can't wait to see the pictures!

I slid the letter back inside the envelope and placed it on the table. It wouldn't be the worst of them—letters full of well wishes for the future and hope for what was to come. Letters filled with love and joy over what our first year must've looked like, with no idea how wrong they would be.

I picked up the next one despite my tears, spying James's handwriting on the front.

Colbie and Phil

I didn't miss the fact that he leaned farther from me when he saw his handwriting, no doubt feeling embarrassed about whatever the letter must contain.

Colbie and Phil,

Happy one year! Wishing you all the best.

Yours,

James Baker

I stiffened, turning my head slightly to stare at him. "Baker? You included your last name?" I laughed through my tears. "Did you honestly think I wouldn't know it was you?"

His smile was halfhearted. "I wasn't sure."

It wasn't just the use of his last name that had bothered me, but the formality and stiffness of the entire letter. The abruptness. I'd expected him to tease me, to mention old memories like he had in his rehearsal dinner toast. But this felt...cold. Off.

Ignoring the feeling, I moved on to the next letter. There were several more from aunts, cousins, coworkers, and friends. More of the same wishes and advice I'd read in Aunt Jean's letter.

I read a letter from my sister, reminding me not to let Phil get away and reminding Phil to always let me have the last slice of cheesecake. There was a letter from my stepdad, saying how much he knew my mom would've loved to be there if she could and how much he loved me. He said Phil was a good man and he hoped we'd be as happy as he'd been with my mom. He'd even included a photo of me wearing my mom's wedding dress as a child, one I knew she'd intended to give me herself if she'd lived to see the day.

When I reached the letter from Phil's parents, I paused, contemplating not reading it at all. I wondered how the letter had ended up in the box in the first place, deciding Aunt Jean must've delivered it for them, since they couldn't be bothered to attend themselves. I hadn't heard from them since the funeral—not a phone call or a text.

I didn't want to read the letter with any bitterness in my heart, though I had little else for the people who were meant to be my in-laws.

Phillip,
We've always loved you and always will.

Your father and I wish you all the happiness in the world. Congratulations to you and your wife on your first anniversary.

We love you, son.

Mom and Dad

I folded the letter, resisting the urge to crumple it up, and reached for the next one.

"That's from me." Eric cleared his throat, rubbing the back of his neck as he eyed the envelope in my hands.

I opened it with care, feeling his stare burning into me.

Phil and Colbie—

I'm sure you've spent the last year arguing over whose best friend I am now. I get it, I get it. But let me assure you—I like you both well enough. Let me go ahead and apologize for any nights I crashed at your place because I was too drunk to find my way home and for any dirty stuff I might've interrupted with an ill-timed text or unannounced visit. What can I say, Colbie? I was in his life first. He'll always love me a little more. Phil, I'm sorry if she's fallen in love with me by this point. Ladies can't help it. I warned you.

Anyway, I love you both. Never thought Phil would find someone to settle him down, but I couldn't have chosen anyone better. Here's to a year of memories, you two, and a lifetime more.

Love you both.

Eric

PS I think it's safe to assume this is still a question I'll need to ask a lot... Can I borrow $20?

I laughed through my tears, shaking my head as he furrowed his brow, leaning over the table to see the letter.

"I don't even remember what I wrote." He scanned the page, a stray tear gliding down his cheek, then he rolled his eyes in spite of himself. "Guess I don't need twenty bucks anymore, do I?" He sniffled, taking another drink of his beer as he sank back into his chair.

"Phil would've been really proud of you." I nodded. "He always wanted you to get your license."

He smiled through his tears. "He said I was going to take him to Hawaii with my first commission check. To pay him back for...well, everything." He shrugged, looking down. "He never thought I'd actually do it."

"That's not true," I assured him, though it partially was. Phil never thought his best friend would decide to focus long enough to get his real estate license, not after years of bouncing from couch to couch and party to party. But he always knew he *could* do it if only he cared to try. "He hoped the wedding would help you settle down."

"Well, he wasn't wrong. He always had a way of making things happen." He eyed the box. "Was that all?

Mosquitoes are eating me up out here." As if to prove a point, he swatted his arm.

James tossed him the bottle of bug spray as I reached in the box for the last letter.

"One more."

This one had no name on the outside of the card, no handwriting for me to try to recognize.

I tore it open, relief over being nearly done settling in my core.

Colbie,

I sucked in an audible breath, ice sliding down my spine. It wasn't possible.

"What's wrong?"

"It's..."

I couldn't find the words. Couldn't find my breath.

If you're reading this, it means I'm already gone.

I'm so sorry about that. It was selfish of me to love you, Colbie. Selfish of me to marry you when I knew what I'd be doing to you. When I knew I couldn't protect you.

It would be selfish of me now to ask you to forgive me, when I don't deserve an ounce of your forgiveness. But that's what I want to do.

I hope I'm still with you by the time you open this letter. I hope that you know the truth about me—who I am and what I've done. And I hope that, by some miracle, I'm still right by your side.

But if I'm not—if I'm gone—if I never see *you again, know how much I loved you. Know* *how badly I wanted to protect you from all of* *this. And know that, with my last breath, I'll* *be thinking of you.*

Love always,

Phil

I hadn't noticed the men leaning forward, trying to get a better look at what I was reading. When Eric saw the name, he reached for the letter, scrambling to read the entire thing.

"Is it really from him?" he asked, his voice cracking.

"I... I think so."

"But what does it mean?" That was James, watching me closely.

"I..." I shook my head. "I don't know."

"He knew he was going to..." Miles was reading the letter with Eric now. "That something was going to happen? How?"

"It's not possible," I said firmly, finding my voice. "Is it?" I was looking at Eric, begging him to tell me I was misreading. Misunderstanding.

He passed the letter back to me, a guarded look in his eyes, and I laid it in front of me, smoothing down the corners. This might have been the last thing my husband touched. I tried to imagine him bent over the page, scribbling this message from...where? His car? His dressing room before the wedding? The letter was at the bottom so it was likely the first to go into the box—unless he'd purposefully placed it at the bottom so it would be the last letter I'd read?

Had he placed it inside while we were setting up? Or during the excruciating wait before the ceremony?

The possibilities were endless and painful.

"How could he have known?" I sniffled, brushing away a tear. "It was an accident. No one could've predicted—"

"Maybe he was sick. Maybe he knew he was having issues with his heart," James offered.

The citronella smell from the candle burned my lungs as a moth fluttered overhead, apparently unaware the candle was meant to be a deterrent.

Sometimes, when you'd been in the darkness for so long, the light was worth the risk.

"He wasn't." Every bit of the pain I felt was present in Eric's tone. "He would've told me."

I couldn't bring myself to focus on anything.

Nothing made any sense.

"Well, apparently he knew something was wrong." James reached for the letter and read a part aloud. "*Know how badly I wanted to protect you from all of this.* All of what?"

I shook my head. "It makes it sound like he was in danger. But...that's ridiculous, isn't it?" I winced as I met Eric's eyes, the pain staring back at me almost unbearable.

He looked down, pinching the bridge of his nose. "Why wouldn't he have just talked to us? It doesn't make sense. Whatever he had going on...whatever he was worried about— I was supposed to be his best friend."

"You were." Now I was consoling him.

"Apparently not." He pushed up from the table, turning away from us and toward the door.

"Eric—" I moved to stand, but he held a hand up.

"I just need a minute. I'm sorry, Colbie, just... A minute. Please."

He disappeared into the house, leaving us in painful silence, and James put a hand on my arm again. "He shouldn't make this all about himself—"

"I loved Phil for two years, James, but Eric loved him their whole lives. It would be like losing you." Just the thought of it brought new tears to my eyes. "Or you losing me. I don't blame him for needing space. I'm not the only one who lost Phil. I get that."

"Regardless, what are you going to do about the letter?" Miles asked, leaning back in his chair.

I turned my attention back to it, wiping sweat from the back of my neck. My wild blonde curls had begun to frizz from the humidity, and I used the ponytail holder from my wrist to tie them back.

"What should I do about it? What *can* I do about it?" I eyed the paper. His last words to me only left me more confused than ever. "Whatever danger he thought he was in, his death was an accident... No one caused it."

"There's no reason to dwell on it," James agreed, moving to fold the letter. "It doesn't change anything." His voice was quieter now, gentle and nearly apologetic.

"I wish it did, but it doesn't. At least... At least you got to hear from him one last time."

But that wasn't enough.

It would never be enough.

I stood, dropping the cards back into the box.

"Where are you going?" James asked as I turned to go inside.

"I just need a minute." It was the understatement of the century, but it was all I could muster. I opened the door and disappeared, cursing myself for waiting a year to read the letters in the first place.

CHAPTER FOUR

"You okay?" I knocked softly on the half-opened door, spying Eric at the desk, bent over his laptop with his cheek resting in his hand.

At the sound of my voice, he closed the laptop and spun around in his chair. He sighed, leaning forward over his knees as I sank onto the end of the bed. "I could ask you the same thing."

I ran my hands over my thighs, looking away from him. "To be honest, I don't know whether to be upset that it took me so long to find the letter, or that I opened that stupid box in the first place."

"You didn't know."

"But now I do. And what am I supposed to do with that?"

He raked a hand through his dark, chocolate-colored hair. "What *can* you do?"

"I just feel like I should...do *something*, you know? It sounds like he knew he was in danger, but—" I cut myself off, rolling my eyes. "I sound ridiculous. Utterly ridiculous."

"You don't sound ridiculous. You sound confused and…and worried. I can't say I blame you."

"What could he have meant, Eric? Why wouldn't he have said anything to us?"

He drew in one side of his mouth, his eyes soft. "I wish I knew. I really, really do."

"Was he…acting weird on the day of the wedding? Did he say anything to you? Or do anything that seemed off?"

He stared off for a moment, obviously thinking back. "No, he was the same old Phil. I mean, he was nervous, sure, but that's to be expected. More than anything…he just kept telling me how happy he was." Tears welled in his eyes and he looked down, inhaling deeply. "How lucky."

I couldn't bring myself to say anything. Couldn't open my mouth for fear I'd break out in sobs again.

So, we sat in silence for what felt like an eternity, the pain and heartbreak in the room palpable as we tried to compose ourselves.

When he looked up, he swiped the back of his arm across his cheek. "He really loved you, you know that? Like…more than I'd ever seen him love anyone."

"Even you?" I teased through my tears.

He nodded, eyes closed. "Even me."

"I loved him too. He was one of the good ones."

"The best."

"I keep trying to think back over that day… I've spent

so much of this year trying not to do that, but now, I want to remember. To see if I'm forgetting something. It's all such a blur for me. I know we talked more than once—but I can't even remember what he said. I've gone over it and over it in my head. The morning was such a rush with trying to get everything there and set up, and dealing with the caterers and photographer... I don't think I actually talked to Phil until later in the day."

"Yeah, by the time I got there—"

"That's right!" My eyes widened. "You were late that day. We were waiting on you to do pictures. I don't think you ever explained why... Did you?"

He looked down. "I don't even remember, to be honest. I was probably hungover."

But there was something in the way he'd shifted. Something in his eyes that had me doubting him.

Was he lying?

Why would he need to?

What did he know?

CHAPTER FIVE

ONE YEAR AGO — WEDDING DAY

"How are you feeling?" James was tapping something into his phone as he walked into the room. When he looked up, his eyes widened. "Wow. You look...wow."

"Thanks." I waved him off, my face half made up, hair finally in place. "I'm not done yet. I knew I should've paid to have someone else do this."

"Er, anything I can help with?"

I laughed. "Not unless you've become a makeup artist without telling me?"

His smile was sheepish. "Can't say I have. Do you want me to grab Amber? Maybe she could—"

"No." My response came too quickly. "No. I'll be fine. I just can't get the wings to match." I pointed toward the eyeliner pen resting on the vanity in front of me, then checked my watch. "Shoot. I'll have to come back and do this in a minute. The caterer should be here any minute, and I'm supposed to be meeting the band. How's the space looking?"

"Good. They've got the chairs all set up now, and they're putting the flower things along each row."

"Awesome. Did you see Phil?"

"He was getting pictures, but I think they're waiting for one of his groomsmen to finish up."

"Which one? What's he doing?"

"Huh?"

"They're waiting on one of his groomsmen to finish doing what?"

His brows drew down, and I realized we were both confused. After a moment, he gasped. "Oh, wait, no. I meant he's waiting on one of his groomsmen to get here. So they can finish up with their pictures. I don't know which one."

I stood from the cushioned stool I'd been sitting on, my skin cold. "What? Are you serious?"

"Uh, yeah. You didn't know?"

I checked my watch again, though I already knew the time. "I had no idea. The wedding starts in four hours. They're supposed to be nearly done with pictures. It's almost our turn."

"What's going on in here?" My sister, Amber, appeared in the doorway, still dressed in the matching silk pajamas I'd bought for the three of us. James had only agreed to wear his long enough for early morning arrival pictures.

"Is someone late?" I demanded. "James said they're waiting on one of the groomsmen."

"It's Eric," Amber said, admiring her nails as if the news wasn't devastating. "Why are you panicking? He'll be here. You know he's probably hungover somewhere, waking up next to a stranger. Or in a ditch." She threw the last part out with a quick roll of her eyes.

"It's our wedding day," I seethed. "It's just one day. That's all I asked. He promised he'd be here on time—"

"He will." James put a hand on my shoulder. "I'll take care of it, okay? I'll go talk to Phil, see what I can do."

The sting of fresh tears filled my eyes.

"Don't cry. You'll mess up your...wings or whatever." James smiled, squeezing my shoulder. "He'll be here. I promise."

With that, he backed away, returning his gaze to his phone. Before Amber or I could say anything else, the door opened again and our wedding planner, Dilma, leaned into the room.

She held a hand up. "I'm sorry to interrupt. I just have a few things to go over with you." She glanced between us. "Do you have a minute?"

I stared at the ceiling, batting my eyelashes and fanning my eyes to keep from ruining the makeup I'd already applied. Then, I turned my attention back to her.

"Let's go."

She seemed unsure, but eventually backed out of the room and pointed toward the long hallway that would lead to our reception area. "I've got the caterer already setting up and the food will be here an hour before we start. The band just arrived, so if you have a minute to go over any last-minute changes to the set list..."

"Sure." I sniffled. Amber was trailing behind us, popping her bubble gum as we walked.

"What the hell did you just say to me?"

I froze at the sound of my soon-to-be husband's voice. At first, I'd thought he might be joking around with his friends, but I quickly realized that wasn't the case. Whoever he was talking to, he was furious.

"You heard me. When are you going to—"

"Who the fuck do you think you are, bro?"

"Yoo-hoo?" Dilma held up a hand, forcing me to stop. She walked forward and peered down a hallway to our left. *"Bride crossing,"* she sang, as if she hadn't just stumbled onto a heated argument. Then again, I assumed she saw all sorts of things in her line of work and was probably used to brushing most things under the rug. "Close your eyes, gentlemen."

After a brief pause, she waved me forward, moving quickly past the hallway. Phil was there, eyes covered dutifully, but it was the other person in the hall that my eyes fell to.

James was red faced, gripping his phone. When he saw me, his worried expression faded. He offered an apologetic smile and a half shrug. Dilma slipped an arm behind my waist—apparently I wasn't moving quickly enough—and rushed me forward.

"Thank you, gentlemen," she called, once we were safely out of their view.

As she walked me through the catering setup, I couldn't bring myself to focus.

What had James and Phil been arguing about?
What on earth could have them so upset?
And where was Eric?

CHAPTER SIX

PRESENT DAY

When I awoke the next morning, James was already up, showered, and dressed.

There was a mug of coffee waiting for me on the nightstand and, when I pushed myself up into a sitting position, he looked up from the book he was reading—a memoir with a dog on the front cover—and offered a lopsided grin. "Mornin', sleepyhead."

"Morning." I groaned, rubbing sleep from my eyes. I checked the time. It was just past six. "You're up early."

"I was going to run into town to get groceries. You want to go?"

"Yeah, of course." I reached for the mug of coffee, taking a cautious sip. "Let me just get dressed."

He placed the book down, sliding toward the edge of his bed. "No rush." He stood, then seemed to think better of it and sat back down. "Are you okay? You were already asleep when I came to bed last night, so we didn't get to talk."

I was out of bed and digging through my suitcase before I answered. "I'm as okay as I can be. I just needed to rest."

"Did you remember to call Jerry before bed?"

I nodded. "He's hanging in there. Starting to sound better."

"Good." He inhaled sharply, something obviously on his mind. "Do you wish Phil had never written you that letter? That you'd never seen it?"

I pressed my lips together, contemplating the question as I tossed a clean shirt and yoga pants over my shoulder before grabbing my face wash. "No. You know, I spent a lot of time last night asking myself that and, at the end of the day, I'm glad I have something from him... A goodbye, of sorts. It makes it harder and more confusing, but I wouldn't change it. I'll take anything I can get from him, even if that means it hurts me a little more."

He was quiet for a moment, his hands gathered in his lap.

"I'm going to get ready, then we can go." I grabbed the mug of coffee and carried it with me, taking another sip as I disappeared into the bathroom.

Moments later, I returned fresh faced, hair pulled back, and dressed. I downed the last of my coffee, still trying to wake up as we walked through the quiet house.

Outside, the humid morning air greeted us. Birds chirped overhead, replacing the usual sounds of morning traffic. I swiped sweat from my upper lip. It was going to be a scorcher.

James slid into the driver's seat of Eric's car as I

searched for my sunglasses in my purse. He started the car, cranking up the air conditioning. "Was your coffee good?"

"To be honest, I'm not sure I tasted it." I laughed. "But I needed it, so thank you." As if to prove a point, I yawned as I hooked my seat belt.

"Well, I know you prefer your *crap*puccinos, but it was the best I could do," he teased, placing a hand on my headrest as he stared over his shoulder to back us down the driveway.

"Excuse you. My *Frap*puccinos are heavenly. They're the only thing to blame for my bright and sunshiny demeanor."

"We have Starbucks to thank for that, do we?"

"Mm-hmm." I pulled my feet up on the dash. "Did you tell Eric we were taking the car?"

"I mentioned it last night. He just said it might need gas. We'll probably be back by the time they wake up anyway."

I nodded, flipping through the radio stations in search of something good to listen to. Giving up, I opened my phone and searched through the music I had downloaded.

"What were you two talking about last night anyway?" James glanced over at me.

"Oh, nothing really. Just...Phil. The letter."

"Does he have any idea what it might've been about?"

I selected an Ed Sheeran album. "No, but we did

start talking about the wedding... Eric was late that day, do you remember that?"

"Yeah. How could I forget?"

"Do you remember why?"

His tone was cautious when he answered. "I don't think he would've told me. We weren't exactly friends back then."

"He doesn't remember either." I patted my legs to the beat of the song.

"Hey, did you listen to the newest episode of the podcast?" He beamed.

"I haven't yet. What's it about?"

"I interviewed that doctor in Australia about animal acupuncture. He had some really interesting things to say about it. I'd never really considered the options out there, but remember I told you about that article of his I read? Supercool stuff."

"Really nice of him to come on."

"Yeah, it was."

I lifted my glasses as the sun disappeared behind a patch of clouds. "Hey, can I ask you something?"

"Sure." He lowered the volume on the radio.

"What do you remember about that day?"

"The wedding?"

"Yeah."

"Um, not a lot, really. It was all such a whirlwind. Why?" He sounded bizarrely defensive.

"No real reason. Eric and I were talking, and I was trying to think back over the day. I remembered over-hearing your fight with Phil."

"Fight?" His brows drew down.

"You don't remember?"

"I mean, I know things got heated between us a few times, just because we were all stressed. I wouldn't exactly call any of it a fight."

"A *few* times? You've never mentioned that before."

"When should I have?" he pressed. His tone was gentle, but I could tell he was annoyed by the way he couldn't bother to look at me.

"Well, what were some of those *heated moments* about?"

He sighed, rubbing his head. "It's been a year, Colbie. The most stressful year of my life. If there's something you want to ask me, just do it. Otherwise, I'd rather not talk about that day if that's okay."

"Why not?"

He rubbed his jaw thoughtfully. "Because every time you think about it, your heart breaks all over again, and I'd rather not be the cause of that today."

"Why won't you tell me what you remember? Something. Anything."

"There's nothing to tell, Colbie. I remember what you remember, okay? I'm... Look, I'm not trying to be difficult, but he's gone. I have no desire to upset you by rehashing how rude I was to your fiancé on your wedding day. I feel awful about it now. And, truthfully, I don't understand why you're putting yourself through this again."

I leaned my head back against the seat. "I just want to

understand what was going through his head when he wrote that letter."

"I wish I knew." His tone was decidedly less harsh then.

"Did you see him fighting—er, having *animated discussions* with anyone else that day?" I elbowed him, trying to lighten the mood.

"No, I didn't. Why are you pushing this? Why are you bringing all of this up now? Do you think that letter had something to do with our fight?"

"Of course not."

"Do you think I did something to hurt Phil? Do you honestly think I'm capable of that?"

"No, James, that's not what I'm saying. I'm just..." I looked away, a sob caught in my throat. After a moment, I spoke again. This time, my voice was softer. "I'm just trying to understand what happened. What he went through on that day. The pain in that letter was very real."

He sighed, and when I looked back, he was gripping the steering wheel tighter, his knuckles white. "Look, your wedding day wasn't my finest moment, as I'm sure you recall." He pressed his lips together. "I wish I could take it all back. Everything I did, everything I said..." The words hung between us, and I knew what he meant without him elaborating. "I was rude to him that day, I said some stuff I can't take back, and it sucks, because he's gone now. And I was a jerk."

My breathing caught. "Do you still mean what you said that day? Do you still believe it?"

He shot a cautious glance my way. "I don't want to speak badly about him. You loved him. What's done is done."

"So, that's a yes."

"Do you really want me to go there? I don't want to fight with you. This weekend was supposed to be relaxing."

"We aren't fighting. I just... I need to know."

He swallowed, nodding slowly. "I meant everything I said that day, yes. I wish it hadn't gone down the way it did. I wish I would've found a better time, a better way, but it was true. He didn't seem to care that you were stressed. He wasn't worried about Eric being there on time. You didn't deserve that. I'm sorry I snapped at him. I feel so guilty for it now, but I don't regret what I said to defend you. I know he's gone and that really sucks because all I wanted was for you to be happy and, if he made you happy, great. But he wasn't at all concerned about something that really bothered you, and that pissed me off."

The argument we had at the wedding flashed in my head.

"I know you think he wasn't good enough for me—"

"It doesn't matter what I think." He twisted his lips. "I was out of line that day, he was right. You both were. It was just a stressful day. I stand by what I said, but it wasn't my place to say it. I'm sorry I did."

"I know you were coming from a good place." I wrung my hands together in my lap. "You were always so protective of me."

"Your mom made me swear I'd take care of you," he said with a soft chuckle. "I take that responsibility very seriously."

"Do you think she would've liked Phil?" The vulnerability in my voice scared me.

He was silent for a beat as we came to a stop at a red light. "I think she would've been happy as long as you were happy."

"If she could only see me now," I whispered, looking away.

"Well, you haven't had your Frappuccino yet."

The joke caught me off guard, and I couldn't help laughing through my tears. I was so grateful for James, for everything he'd ever done for me, and for the way he seemed to know exactly what I needed to hear without me laying it out for him.

We rode in silence the rest of the way, the music nearly lulling me back to sleep as I thought back to my wedding day.

I'd spent so much of the last year avoiding thinking about it, but now, I couldn't seem to get it off my mind.

CHAPTER SEVEN

WEDDING DAY

"Are you ready?" Amy, our photographer, asked as she held her hand up to stop me from walking any farther.

Up ahead, with his back to me, Phil nodded. "I've been ready."

She grinned, getting her camera in place. "Turn around and see your bride."

He spun to face me slowly, his eyes squeezed shut, and as he did, I began to walk toward him. When he opened his eyes, mine began to water.

He grinned at me with a warm, proud expression. As I drew nearer, he held his hands out, ready to welcome me. I'd never felt more beautiful or loved than in that moment.

It was as if the sky had opened up and I'd walked straight toward the sun. The warmth that spread throughout my body was unlike anything I'd ever felt.

"You look..." He covered his mouth, tears filling his

own eyes. "You look beautiful."

Though it seemed impossible, heat warmed my cheeks even more as we closed the space between us. The clicking sounds of the camera and crunching of Amy's footsteps in the dry grass were forgotten—fading away like white noise as we lost ourselves in each other's eyes.

"I love you." I leaned close to him, so happy my heart felt as if it were going to explode.

He swiped a tear from his cheek. "I can't believe you're going to be my wife." As he leaned down and pressed a kiss to my lips, I breathed in the scent of him—smoky and woodsy. No moment had ever felt so full of love and happiness and hope.

When he pulled back, almost regrettably, his forehead came to rest on mine as Amy circled around us, clicking away. I couldn't bring myself to care about whether she was getting the shots we'd talked about. All I could think about—all I could see—was Phil. The man I was going to marry. The man I was going to love for the rest of my life.

"I love you," I whispered again. It was all I could bring myself to say. My brain was a whirlwind of emotions, very little making sense to me at that moment. He seemed to sense it—maybe mistaking it for panic—and wrapped his arms around me. He smoothed a hand over my back, lowering his mouth to my ear. Even with our audience, even as the moment was captured on camera for the world to see, it felt as intimate as it had ever been. As if no one else existed in the universe, let alone this place.

"It's going to be okay," he vowed, his breath warm on my cheek. The sensation sent goose bumps down my arms. "I'm going to take care of you forever. You know that, right? I'll never let anything bad happen to you. Never let you get hurt." He inhaled deeply, his nose pressed into my hair. "You're safe with me, Colbie."

"I love you," I repeated the words for the third time, just before Amy approached us.

"I've got some great ones, guys. Do you need a minute, or are we ready to move on to the group ones?"

Snapping back to reality, I wiped a tear from my eye, keeping an arm wrapped around his waist.

Phil turned his attention to her. "I think we're ready—"

"Actually, could we have just a minute?"

Amy and Phil both appeared taken aback as I asked the question. In truth, I'd shocked myself, not fully prepared for the conversation I wanted to have. I didn't want the happiness of the moment to dissipate.

"Of course." Amy stepped back and pointed to the building behind us. "I'll just be right inside getting a few more pictures of the venue. Let me know when you're ready, and I'll bring the group out here."

Once she'd disappeared inside, the cloudy sky reflecting on the glass of the door as she shut it, I turned back to Phil. His sly grin was contagious.

"There's a shed down by the gardens if you're looking for a quickie." He winked, pulling me into him.

I chuckled, placing my hands on his chest. "Nice try, but if you mess up my makeup, I might have to kill you."

He kissed my forehead. "Fair enough for now. Is... everything okay?"

"I think so."

"That doesn't sound okay." He gripped both my hands between our chests. "What's going on?"

"Actually, that's what I wanted to ask you."

His thumbs rubbed over my knuckles, his touch making it hard to concentrate when every nerve in my body was begging to hug him again, to move closer. He tilted his head to the side.

"I heard you earlier. When you were with James in the hallway. It...sounded like you were fighting. Is everything okay?"

He was still for a moment, thinking perhaps, and then his expression softened. "I was hoping you hadn't heard that. I'm so embarrassed."

"Why? Why were you fighting? What happened?"

"Nothing." His response was quick. Clipped. "I promise you, it's nothing."

"It didn't sound like nothing."

"It's nothing for you to worry about." He tucked his hand under my chin, bringing my mouth up to meet his. Seconds before our lips connected, he whispered, "I don't want you to worry about anything today. It's just you and me."

He pressed our lips together, forcing me to forget what we'd said seconds ago, to forget all my worries, to forget everything.

He was good at that.

CHAPTER EIGHT

PRESENT DAY

I shoved my hand into the freezing cold water of the cooler, shifting the ice around in search of a bottle of beer.

"Get me one, will ya?" Eric glanced at me with one eye squinted shut from the blazing sun, a metal spatula in his hand. The smoke from the grill overwhelmed me as he opened it, the tantalizing scent of the charcoal and burgers causing my stomach to rumble. I pulled two bottles from the cooler, shaking my hands off and passing him a beer before drying my hands on my shirt.

I sat down in the red metal chair, crossing one leg over the other as I heard a splash from the pool. Glancing through the slats of the porch, I spied Miles swimming laps, the chiseled muscles of his tan back rippling with each move.

"If he spends any more time in there, he's going to forget how to walk on land," Eric mumbled.

I turned my attention back to him, twisting the lid off

my drink. "At least someone's getting some use out of it." I swatted a mosquito from my arm. "How are the burgers looking?"

"Nearly done." He flipped the last one, scooting it over on the aluminum foil, and shut the lid, hanging the spatula on the empty holder attached to the side of the grill. "Hungry?"

"Starving." I placed my bottle on the table, spinning it around between my fingers, the places I'd touched clearly decipherable in the condensation. "How're you feeling this morning?"

"I'm okay." He paused, tossing the lid to his beer across the table. "You?"

I was silent for a moment, weighing what I wanted to tell him next. He would tell me it was a terrible idea, I knew. And he was probably right.

"I want to talk to Phil's parents."

He practically spat his drink out, his eyes wide. "You *what?* Why?"

"I've been thinking about it and...it feels like the right thing to do. Maybe they can help me clear up what he might've been talking about. Maybe they can help ease my mind because right now...I'm spiraling. Questioning everything. It seems like Phil knew something bad was going to happen to him, and until I can get a better understanding of what was going on in his head that day, I'm not going to be able to let it go."

He eased down in the chair next to me. "I get it. Really, I do. But...his parents aren't going to help you. You know that. They wouldn't even help me." What he was leaving unspoken was clear—*they don't hate me like they hate you*.

"I know that, but don't you think they deserve to know? I mean, all this time we've thought Phil's death was an accident, but—"

"Phil's death *was* an accident, Colbie. The police said so. The doctors said so. Why are you putting yourself through this? Whatever he was talking about—if he was talking about anything—none of that had to do with why he died. We both know that. All dredging up the past will do is break your heart even more."

"But what if we're wrong? What if we should've looked harder? What if something happened and we didn't even look into it? Don't you want to know? Doesn't he deserve that?"

"He had a heart attack, Colbie."

"*I know that.*" My tone was too sharp. Too biting. He didn't deserve my anger when he was one of the only things that had kept me standing over the past year.

"I'm sorry—"

"No, I'm sorry. I don't mean to snap at you—"

"It's fine—"

"It's just... He was healthy. He was young and active and in perfect health. So, why? Why would he have a heart attack out of nowhere? Why on our wedding day of all days?"

"He had a stressful job. A stressful family. The doctors said—"

"*Healthy thirty-year-olds don't just drop dead with no warning signs.*" I was shouting again. It was the same thing I'd told the doctors, but it hadn't mattered. No one was listening to me then, just like no one was listening to me now. I squeezed my eyes shut, tuning out the noise. Tears streamed down my cheeks and he pulled me into his chest, both arms around my neck.

He sighed, his breath hot on my cheek. Goose bumps covered my skin. "I know. It doesn't make sense. I've asked myself that question every day since it happened." His lips brushed my temple, a gesture I wasn't sure he realized he'd made.

We were still for a moment. I closed my eyes, resting my forehead on his shoulder. I wished I could let it go. Logically, it made sense what he was saying. Logically, I knew what the doctors had said. They'd done all they could do, but his heart had just given out. It was a random tragedy. They were sorry for my loss. At the time, I was numb with disbelief. I hadn't thought to question it further than questioning why something awful would happen. Why me? Why him?

Until opening that letter, the idea that something *else* might've happened, that someone might've wanted to hurt Phil had never occurred to me.

"Everyone loved him."

"I know." Eric pulled back slightly, meeting my eyes.

I hadn't even realized I'd said it out loud. "He was so..." Unable to bring myself to say more, to attempt to put into words just how special, perfect, kind, and loving Phil was, I dropped my head.

"He was *so*..." Eric agreed. "But you are, too. And that's why I can't let you go through with this. I can't let them hurt you or insult you... You don't deserve the way they've treated you."

"They lost their son—"

"And you were meant to be their daughter. You lost someone too. You didn't deserve for them to abandon you."

"It's not that simple." I pursed my lips.

"It was for me. He was my best friend. I could've walked away after he died, but I didn't."

"Why didn't you?" I pulled back slowly, wanting to meet his eyes fully as I asked the question. I'd never gotten an official answer to this one.

"Because..." He looked away, his jaw tight, unwilling to meet my eye. "Because it's what he would've wanted."

I was slow to nod, but eventually, I did. "Is that the only reason?"

"I..." His eyes landed on mine finally, darting back and forth. "I mean, it's—"

"Dinner done?" The screen door swung open and James appeared in the doorway, a book in his hand. We jolted apart as if we'd been caught doing something wrong. Heat crept up my neck.

Eric shot up from his chair, moving to check the burgers again. "Just about."

"Everything okay?" James shut the door behind him, moving closer to me with a worried stare.

Eric started to answer for me. "Fine—"

"I'm thinking of going to talk to Phil's parents."

James sank down in the chair Eric had just been occupying. "What? Why?"

"They deserve to know about the letter. And...I'm hoping they can give me some reassurance or insight about what he may have been talking about."

"Are you sure that's a good idea? They haven't exactly been...er, kind." James winced.

"Understatement of the century," I heard Eric mumble behind me.

"I don't know whether it's a good idea, but I have to do something. I'm going to go crazy if I just sit here and stew over it. If I go and talk to them and they send me away or refuse to listen, at least I'll know. At least I tried. But it's been a year. Maybe they want to talk to me as much as I want to talk to them. And, if not, if they can at least answer some of my questions...any of my questions... I'm hoping it will help me move on."

James dog-eared a page of the book in his hand and leaned forward over his knees. "If you've made up your mind, I'll go with you. You shouldn't go alone."

Before I could respond, a hand gripped my shoulder. "She's already asked me."

James's gaze shot up to meet Eric's.

"I should be the one to go with her." James's voice was firm.

"Agree to disagree. You don't know them like I do, and she asked me first." Eric released my shoulder. "I know how to handle them."

"So you'll go with me? Really?" I turned to face him, shielding my eyes from the sun.

"If that's what you want, yes."

I couldn't bear to meet James's eyes. I knew he

61

wanted me to choose him, but for this mission, Eric was the best candidate. "Okay, thank you."

He saluted me with the spatula before beginning to pull the burgers from the grill, a small grin playing at the corners of his mouth. "I'll take care of her."

It wasn't clear whether he was talking to James, or perhaps to Phil, but either way, I couldn't suppress the relief I felt. Relief combined with bubbles of worry.

I was going to get to the bottom of this. Really, I was.

If you were trying to tell me something, babe, tell me now. Help me find the truth.

CHAPTER NINE

WEDDING DAY

"Knock knock." He said the words, rather than actually knocking as the door opened.

I spun around in my seat, spying Jerry in the doorway. He was the most dressed up I'd ever seen him—having traded in his usual grease-covered overalls and baseball cap for a tux and side-slicked hair. Tears welled in my eyes at the sight of him. At the effort.

"Hi."

He smiled, his red, wrinkled chin quivering. "Hi." He shook his head, one hand over his mouth. "Your momma would be so proud of you."

The tears spilled over onto my cheeks, matching the tears on his. "I wish she could be here."

"I wish she could too, kiddo." He pulled me into a hug, and I melted into his arms. This wasn't how my wedding day was supposed to go. As a young girl, when I pictured this day, never once did I think my parents might not be here. Or that the only parental figure I'd

63

have would be the man who stepped in when I was a teenager, who saw me only at my worst. The man I'd pushed away for so many years.

Now, he was all I had left.

I didn't deserve him.

"Thank you for coming." I inhaled deeply as I pulled away, dusting my cheeks.

"Ah, I wouldn't have missed it for the world. You know that." He locked eyes with me, his head tilting toward his shoulder.

"You look great. Is the tux okay?"

"Yeah, it's fine." He tugged at his jacket absentmindedly. "You know, I'll be glad to get back into my jeans, but it's real nice all the same. I just keep worrying I'll get something on it."

"The cleaning is covered in the rental." I sniffled. "So don't worry about that."

He seemed as if he wanted to say something, his mouth opening, then closing thoughtfully.

"Everything okay?"

Without a word, he reached into his jacket pocket and pulled out a white envelope.

"What's this?" I reached for the envelope, recognizing the faint cursive instantly. New tears stung my eyes.

"Your mom wanted you to have it on your wedding day. If..." He cleared his throat. "If she wasn't here to give it to you herself."

"Oh." Heat rushed to my face, my temples throbbing.

I couldn't bring myself to say anything else for fear of breaking down.

"There's one for Amber on hers too, but I haven't told her yet. I was going to wait to give yours to you after...so I didn't mess up your makeup. But she made me promise to give it to you and, well—"

"It's perfect." I clutched it to my chest. "You've had it all this time?"

"She wrote it right after she got sick." He glanced out the window, tears gleaming in his kind eyes as the corners pinched together, wrinkles deepening. "I never thought I'd actually have to give it to you. I told her then it was a waste of time."

"None of us knew." The pain was palpable in the room. His. Mine. It was unbearable, even now. Years later. That kind of pain never goes away. Never lessens. It lingers and builds, smacking into you at the most random times. "Not even her."

He reached out and squeezed my hand. "She always wanted to make sure you girls knew how much she loved you. How proud she was of you. Especially today. And... I love you too. I'm so proud of you. So happy for you. You look so much like her on...on our wedding day." His words were broken up with sobs as he moved his hand from mine and up to my cheek. "I know I'm not your dad, but that doesn't mean I don't think of you girls like you're my kids. I always have."

I couldn't take it anymore. I threw myself into his arms, sobs threatening to tear through my chest. "You'll always be our Papa Jerry. And I'm glad you're here."

He smoothed a hand over the back of my dress with a drawn-out sigh. When he pulled back, he wiped tears from his eyes with both hands, looking me over proudly. There was so much unspoken between us—apologies, memories, and heartache. "I don't wanna mess up your hair or makeup. It's supposed to be a happy day. I'm going to go out here and see if anyone needs any help."

"Jerry?"

He stopped moments before he reached the door. "Yeah?"

"Do you... Do you think Mom would've liked Phil?"

"Oh, honey." He stepped back toward me, a calloused hand reaching for my arm. "She would've loved anyone you love." His expression grew dry. "Why? Did something happen? Do I need to pull the stepdad card?"

I chuckled, giving him a look. "No, nothing like that. I was just... I wish she could've met him."

"I wish she could've too." He kissed my forehead, then turned back toward the door and, with a final nod, retreated from the room.

I glanced down at the envelope in my hand, now creased from my grip. I smoothed my fingers over her handwriting then crossed the room to sit down on the pale-pink couch.

Whatever the letter said, it was sure to both break my heart and bring me peace.

I wanted to savor it. To read it for hours on end.

When my dad passed away, there was no warning. The car wreck that took him from us was sudden and left him with injuries that couldn't be fixed. There had been no time to prepare. No time to say goodbye. No time to tell him everything I'd ever wanted to tell him.

At ten years old, it was the biggest heartbreak of my life.

So, when my mom got sick just after my sixteenth birthday, two years after marrying Jerry, I'd told myself it was better this way. I'd have a chance to say goodbye to her. We'd be able to prepare. She'd find a way to help me through this somehow.

And she had, she'd prepared me in terms of what to do with her will and life insurance and bank accounts, but when it came to saying goodbye, there was really no amount of time that could accurately prepare me for the devastation.

At eighteen years old, one month before my high school graduation, I said goodbye to the only parent I had left. Nothing in the world can prepare you for that.

But now, I had a final chance for a goodbye I hadn't been prepared for. Once I opened this letter, it was really it. Really over.

The last time I would ever hear from her.

I needed weeks, not minutes, to process my feelings surrounding opening it. I wasn't ready to say goodbye again. But, at the same time, my impatience and hope wouldn't allow me to wait a second longer.

I tore open the letter slowly, inch by inch, trying to preserve the envelope, and eased the letter out as if it were made of delicate lace rather than paper.

Unfolding it twice, I sucked in a breath, gulped down a sob, and began to read.

Colbie,

It's Momma. I know you know that, but it breaks my heart to think about how long it might've been since you've heard those words.

I hope this letter makes its way to you, sweet girl. Jerry promises it will. Please be kind to him, Colbie. He loves you. He worries about you. I know he can't replace your father. I know your feelings about me remarrying are complicated, but please don't take that out on him. If you haven't made up by now, I hope you'll consider it.

But I'm not here to lecture you, baby girl. This letter is because it's your wedding day!!!

I can't believe it.

I remember watching you and your sister dress up in your little bride dresses and walk around the house with bouquets you'd picked yourselves.

We've dreamed of this day all your life.

I'm so sorry I'm not there to see it.

I'm so sorry for the sadness you must feel over that. But I hope you know I'm there. In whatever way I can be, I'm there with you today, Colbie. Today and every day.

If I can send you a sign today, I will.

I hope the man you're marrying knows how lucky he is. I hope he knows what a special girl he's got in you. I hope he makes you laugh in the way that makes your nose wrinkle until you snort. I know you hate that, but it's always been one of my favorite things. I hope he takes you to late-night premieres of your favorite movies. I hope he lets you choose the music on road trips. I hope he never makes you feel insecure or less than perfect. I hope he knows how loved you are and were, long before he came along, and I hope he doesn't take that for granted.

I could go on and on, sweet girl, but the doctors keep coming in and giving me strange looks for blubbering over this paper, so I should go.

Congratulations on your wedding and your marriage. I hope you'll be as happy as I was with your father and then again with Jerry. Finding someone special to share a life with... that's all life is really about.

When you're feeling lonely, just remember I'm always with you. Give your sister a hug from me.

Love you,
Momma

I read over the letter twice, both overwhelmed by all she'd said and somehow hoping for more. Hoping it would never end.

A knock at the door interrupted my silent tears, and I stood, dusting my cheeks and clearing my throat. I placed the letter on the coffee table in front of me.

"Come in."

Dilma stood in front of me, tapping something into the tablet in her hand. "Am I interrupting?"

"Nope." I sniffled. "What's up?"

At the sound of my voice, she looked up, her eyes narrowing in a no-nonsense way that said, *No one makes a bride cry under my watch.* "What happened?"

"These are happy tears." I waved her off, not sure whether it was a lie. "It's fine."

Her tablet chimed, and she glanced down. "Are you sure?"

"Positive."

"Everything's going exactly according to plan. If you have a minute, the band just arrived, and I want you both to meet them."

"Sure." I wiped my cheeks again.

"You'll have to tell me what setting spray you used." She grinned, moving across the room to lead me out. "Because it is working wonders." I couldn't tell if she was being genuine, but a quick glance in the mirror told me my makeup had—for the most part—held up quite well.

Thank God for that, because I was a blubbering mess.

We made it out of the room and toward the reception hall, and Dilma stopped us in front of the table where Phil and I would sit in just a few hours for our first meal as husband and wife.

She clicked her tongue, glancing around. "They were supposed to meet us here. Let me see what the holdup is. Stay here, okay?"

I nodded, running my fingertips across the white linen tablecloth. It almost didn't seem real that this was happening.

That this was all for me.

I picked up the place card in front of my plate that read, **Mrs. Phillip Tanner.** I'd never liked the idea of taking his last name officially. We'd debated the idea—he thought it was important, while I thought it was a dated notion. I didn't want to lose such a special part of my identity. To cut ties with such a huge connection to my past. To my family. My parents had only had two girls, which meant our name would die with my sister and me unless one of us kept it.

The compromise had been that, at least for the wedding, I'd go through with tradition, and then legally, we could make the decision at a later date.

I couldn't decide whether the butterflies in my stomach were from joy at seeing the *Mrs.* label for the first time or pain at realizing I'd already made my decision. Seeing it there in black and white made it clear I could never actually go through with the name change.

I only hoped I could make him understand.

"You must be the bride." A smooth, deep voice behind me caused me to jump, and I spun around instantly. It was the kind of voice you'd expect to hear on the radio—crisp and clear, every syllable perfectly enunciated. There was no lazy Southern tongue like I was used to hearing.

The man in front of me was tall and muscular—not beefy, but fit—dressed in a dark suit, with shoulder-length brown hair tied back in a bun and enchanting jade eyes that seemed to light up when he smiled.

Heat radiated to my temples.

"Um, how'd you know?" I motioned to my dress with a laugh that sounded too loud to my own ears.

"Lucky guess." He chuckled and held out his hand. "I'm Miles. The lead singer of Divorced September."

I dropped my brows. "Is that a good name for a wedding band?"

He winced. "Probably not. I think our agent is going to make us change it, to be honest. But, hey, you hired us, so there's hope."

"Well, Dilma just played me a few tracks and I picked the best one. I'm not sure if she mentioned your name."

"Are you superstitious?" He'd moved a step closer to me, though I wasn't sure he even realized it. The room was too small, too hot. I could hardly catch my breath. He was painfully handsome.

"Not entirely."

"Well, if it makes you feel any better, both of our guitar players have been married for years. So, I don't think we're bringing any bad luck to your marriage."

"I'm glad to hear that. What about you?" I had no idea why I was asking. It didn't matter. It was none of my business. Why was he so handsome?

"What? Am I married?"

"Mm-hmm." I ran a finger across the lace of my dress, trying to draw my attention away from his eyes.

"Nah. I'm not the type."

"What does that mean?"

"I mean, marriage is cool if that's your thing…"

"Can it be someone's *thing*?"

"My rent relies on it being a whole lotta people's thing."

"But not yours?"

"Definitely not mine."

I flicked my eyes back up to meet his. "Maybe you just haven't met the right person."

He grinned. "I've met a lot of people."

"And here we are!" Dilma's singsong voice came from behind Miles, and he glanced over his shoulder, not completely turning away from me. "I see you've already met our bride. Here's the groom, Phillip Tanner." She gestured to Phil, and he flashed a charming grin, slipping an arm around my waist before extending his hand to Miles.

Miles visibly stiffened at the sight of him, the warmth disappearing from his expression in an instant. He was cold. A fortress. Something was wrong.

"Hey, man. Super excited to hear you all play."

Seemingly shocked back to reality, Miles raised his hand, holding it out to Phil with a quick shake.

"Where is the rest of the band?" Dilma asked.

"On the way," Miles mumbled, looking directly at her. He would no longer look my way, which shouldn't have bothered me but most definitely did. "I should go get set up."

"Of course," Phil said. "Don't let us get in your way." He gave a politician's laugh, his smile wide and gracious as he patted Miles on the back. "And just let me know if you need anything."

Once Miles had disappeared, Dilma pointed down the hall. "We should get you back to the lounge. Phillip, where are the rings? The photographer has been asking for them."

"My assistant's bringing them. Along with the boutonnieres." He patted the space on his chest where it should've gone.

Dilma's eye twitched with stress. "I hadn't realized we were still waiting on those. We should really get them on." She checked her watch. "Do you have an ETA?"

"Any minute now." He was casual and cool as ever.

"Right. Okay. I'll just go and check on...everything else." She smiled broadly, walking away from us with short, quick steps that made me fear for anyone in her path. She was the best at what she did, which made her terrifying when she needed to be.

"So, that was weird, hmm?" I turned to face Phil.

"Yeah, I think she's more worried about our wedding than we are." He laughed.

"I meant Miles."

"Who?" His brows shot up.

"The singer." I pointed over my shoulder. "Do you know him or something?"

"What?" He followed my finger. "No. I don't think so. Why?"

"You didn't think he was acting strange just now?"

"Uh, no?" His lips remained in an O shape as he watched me, trying to understand. "Was he?"

"You don't know him? You haven't met before?"

He studied Miles again from afar. "I mean, I meet a lot of people, but no. He doesn't look familiar." He pulled me in, wrapping an arm around my shoulders. "What's gotten into you? Pre-wedding nerves?"

"I guess so."

"I know the best way to deal with those." His hand slipped down my back just before he gripped my bottom gently. Then, he pulled me away, leading me back toward the dressing room, and I cast a final glance over my shoulder.

To my surprise, Miles was watching us depart.

Rather, he was watching me.

CHAPTER TEN

PRESENT DAY

"Nap time?" Miles asked, walking around behind me as I yawned.

I was outstretched on the pool deck, propped up with my hands behind my back, my feet dangling in the water. I grinned at him through the yawn. "Just about."

"Where'd they go?" He jutted his head toward the house.

"Eric's working on an offer for a client, and James is taking a shower, I think."

"And you're sitting down here all alone?" He eased himself down next to me, cross-legged and tan. His hair fell around his head without any sense of reason, strands bleached by the sun and dried by the chlorine from earlier.

"I'm not alone now."

"Fair enough." He tucked a strand of hair behind his ear to get a better look at me. "Having a good time so far?"

"Yeah, I guess so. It's been nice to get away."

He stared at me, seeming to sense I wanted to say more, though I wouldn't. Not yet.

"Are you already dreading going back to work on Wednesday?"

"From the moment Friday ended."

He shook his head. "I don't understand working a job you hate. Why don't you just find something else?"

"We can't all be rock stars, Miles. Besides, I don't hate my job. I love seeing the pups and getting to spend time with them."

"You love cutting dogs' hair all day?"

"It beats stocking shelves or sweeping floors—both of which I've done—yeah. For the most part, it's just me and the dogs. No other people. I like that."

"You don't like people?" He lowered his voice, nudging his shoulder into mine playfully.

"Not all people, anyway."

"Well, for the record, I think you'd make an excellent rock star."

At that, I giggled, tossing my head back. "Trust me, I wouldn't. The dogs I work with don't even like my singing."

He was still for a moment, studying me. "Hey, why don't you have a dog of your own?"

"Hmm?" The question caught me off guard, though it wasn't the first time I'd been asked.

"I've always wondered. James loves animals and has, like, what...eight dogs or something?"

"Three," I corrected.

"But you don't have any."

"I had a dog growing up, but then I couldn't bring her with me in my first apartment, so she stayed with Jerry until she passed away."

"I'm really sorry." There was a grim twist to his mouth.

"Thanks. I, um, I met Phil shortly after, and he's allergic to—he *was* allergic to them. So, once we were serious, it just never made sense for me to get one if I hoped we had any sort of future."

He eyed me skeptically. "His allergies weren't bothered by the dog hair from your work?"

"I'd always shower before I saw him, and wash my clothes. He always wanted me to quit—we didn't need the money—but I planned to wait until we had kids. I'd get bored easily, otherwise."

His expression turned stoic, a far-off look in his eyes.

"Hey, speaking of Phil..." I saw my opening and needed to take it. "Did you...know him? Before the wedding, I mean?"

He cocked his head to the side. "What?"

"When Dilma introduced you to him that day, you were...standoffish, I guess. It made me think maybe you knew him before. That you guys had met."

"Well, did you ask him?"

I pressed my lips together. "Yeah, but he said he didn't know you."

He was slow to nod, his head rising steadily and then falling at a snail's pace. "Well, that's that then."

"So you didn't know him?"

"Why are you asking me this now, Colbie? Why are you asking at all? Does it matter whether I knew him?"

"I guess it doesn't. I'm just... I'm trying to understand."

"To understand what?"

I weighed my words carefully. "I think there are things about Phil that maybe I don't know. Things I don't understand."

"Because of the letter." It wasn't a question.

"That, among other things."

"Like what?" He splashed his feet lazily in the pool next to mine, the cool water keeping me grounded when my emotions threatened to get the best of me. The constant chirp of crickets in the woods was practically deafening.

"Well, the way you acted when you met him, for one thing. And James fought with him that day too. It just seems like everyone saw a side of him I didn't see."

He leaned forward further, his stomach pressing into his thighs as he rubbed his hands together, no longer looking at me. "Well, yeah, but James fighting with him on your wedding day isn't exactly surprising."

His words sent a strange sensation through me, like Jell-O slipping through my core. "What do you mean?"

"Well..." The expression on his face when he met my gaze told me he thought it was obvious. "Watching the best friend you're in love with marrying some other guy isn't exactly a walk in the park for anyone, is it?"

My body went cold, the Jell-O sensation seeming to swell so every part of me was moving in slow motion.

"He's... James isn't in love with me. Don't be ridiculous."

"Yes. He is." He said it so casually, like he hadn't just dropped a bombshell set to implode my life. Then he pressed his hands onto the side of the pool, pushing forward and launching himself into the water.

When he resurfaced, brushing his hair back out of his eyes, I was staring at him in what felt like horror. "James is my best friend. He's been my best friend for as long as I can remember. That's it. I hate when people act as if men and women can't be friends without some sort of romantic feelings being involved."

He moved closer in the water, stopping just in front of me. "Men and women *can* be friends without romantic feelings."

"Thank you."

"You and James can't."

"Stop saying that."

"It's true, Colbie. You know it, even if you don't want to admit it. He's in love with you. My guess is he's been in love with you for a long-ass time."

I scoffed, looking away. It was the most absurd thing I'd ever heard. "Has he told you that?"

"He doesn't have to."

"But... It doesn't make any sense. He's never mentioned it to me."

"Because he's scared to lose you." He stepped forward again, his chest brushing my knees. I stopped moving my feet in the water. "Can't say I blame him."

Heat spread throughout my core, evaporating the

Jell-O in an instant. Was it true? It couldn't be. I refused to believe it. "So... You think that's why they were fighting? Because he..." I checked over my shoulder, lowering my voice, though the chorus of crickets was certainly keeping our conversation private. "Because he has feelings for me? If Phil knew that, why wouldn't he have told me?"

"Maybe he was scared you'd choose James." He shrugged one shoulder.

"What?"

"Would you have?"

"I..." I shook my head, willing the words to come out, but they wouldn't. In truth, it was impossible to know what I would've done. Did I love James? Not in that way. Not as far as I knew.

"Exactly." Miles stared at me, his brows drawn down with intense concentration. I focused on the droplets of water on his skin, his eyelashes, his hair. "If I was in his position, I wouldn't have said anything either."

"I..."

"So, the question remains, do you love him back?"

I looked down, clutching my hands in front of me. "He's my best friend."

"You didn't answer the question."

My pulse pounded in my head, my mind spinning with possibilities.

"Everything okay?"

I jumped, though Miles remained steady as we turned to face Eric. He scrutinized us, a worried look on his face.

"Everything's fine." I cleared my throat as I felt Miles moving farther away from me. "We were just about to go for a swim. Want to join us?"

Eric checked over his shoulder. "I was going to start gathering firewood for the firepit. Any chance you want to help?"

He was looking directly at me, but it was Miles who climbed out of the pool—not bothering to use the stairs. "You got it, chief."

He wrapped a towel around himself, holding out a hand to help me to my feet. I took it, standing and grinning at them both, my face radiating an embarrassed heat as I slipped past Eric.

What did I have to be embarrassed about?

And why were things suddenly so complicated between us all?

AN HOUR LATER, the fire was blazing and the sun had finally begun to set. We sat around the firepit—Miles, James, and Eric were kicked back in yellow, wooden lounge chairs, and I was in the slightly dingy, mostly faded egg chair. Despite the worn state of it, the cushion had proven to be one of the most comfortable things I'd ever sat on. I tucked my legs up under me, rubbing them as the evening chill set in.

"These mosquitoes are eating me alive." Eric swatted one from his calf, as if to prove a point.

"Welcome to the woods." James chuckled, taking a drink of his beer.

"This isn't the woods. It's a freaking subdivision." Eric rolled his eyes, checking his phone.

"In the middle of the woods." That was Miles, mumbling more to himself than anyone else.

"How'd your offer go, Eric?" I desperately wanted to change the subject. Everyone seemed to be on edge since we'd left for this trip, and I couldn't help wondering if I was imagining it or if something was going on.

"We're still waiting to hear. They have twenty-four hours, but it's a solid offer. The other agent said they've had three others come in since the open house, so it's just about who has the better number right now."

"I'm sure they'll get it."

"It's my clients' sixth offer, so there's a lot riding on this one. If they don't get it, I think they'll fire me. The dude's hotheaded already."

"That's crazy. It's not your fault the market's so insane right now."

"Yeah, well..." He slipped his phone back into his pocket. "Tell that to half my clients."

"That's why we choose to work with animals instead of people." James leaned forward to stoke the fire, grinning at me.

"Do pets frequently come in unaccompanied, then?" Miles asked with a wry smile.

"Funny."

"You're right, though." I gave James an encouraging

nod. "It's easier. I could never do what you do, Eric. All that pressure would give me hives."

His gaze fell to me, the shadows making his face seem edgier. Nothing but sharp angles and dark eyes. "It's not so bad."

"No?"

"Nah. I mean, for the most part it's kind of fun. The stressful parts are worth it."

"I need another beer." James stood, walking across the deck. "Anyone else?"

"I'll take one." Miles held up his empty bottle.

"Me too."

"Me three." I tossed my bottle into the trash can behind me. As James walked away, I caught Miles's gaze from across the fire. There was a challenge in his eyes I recognized from earlier, an unspoken conversation happening between us that had been left unfinished.

"Where's your head at?" A smile slowly crept to his lips.

"All over the place." At least I was being honest.

"Everything okay?" Eric asked, glancing between us.

"Just fine." Miles never took his eyes off me.

"Blondie?" Eric pressed.

"I'm okay." I broke eye contact to look his way. "Honest. Just conflicted about everything."

"About going to see his parents?"

"Whose parents?" Miles asked.

"Phil's." We answered at the same time.

"Which, for the record, I still think is a bad idea." James was back. He passed around our drinks, handing me mine last. When he did, his fingers lingered on mine for half a second.

Was that on purpose?

I'd never before been aware of moments between us. Things were so easy before.

Now, Miles had gotten into my head and everything was all messed up.

"I agree," Eric mumbled.

"Why is it a bad idea?" Though Miles had been around quite a bit since the wedding, I'd spared him the dramatic details of my life and almost marriage, which meant he didn't know about my almost-in-laws. I was never sure what to call them. Once, they'd been set to become some of the closest things I had to parents, at least legally. Now, they were strangers with a shared tragedy.

"Because they're evil incarnate." Eric sat back in his chair, twisting the lid off his beer with ease.

Miles looked at me. "What's he talking about?"

"They don't like me."

"But you're their daughter-in-law."

"I was supposed to be, sure, but in their eyes, that's probably the one positive thing that came out of Phil's death. They didn't like me before—not when we were dating and not after we got engaged—and they certainly don't like me now."

"They treated her like crap the entire time she dated Phil. Would never let her come to family holidays, would never include her in anything." Eric's lips flattened, his tone harsh.

"And what would happen?" Miles asked. "When they didn't let you go?"

"I just...wouldn't go."

"He went without you?" Miles spoke through a tight jaw.

"He didn't have a choice." That was Eric, always quick to defend him. "There was no saying no to the Tanners." He tipped back his beer, his words bitter. "Never. Not even when we were kids. They were manipulative. Believe me, he tried to stand up for her when it happened. He got in more fights with them over it than I could count." He nodded at me. I'd heard enough stories from Eric and Phil to know that was true, but it didn't make it sting any less.

"Still, that's kind of bullsh—"

"It doesn't matter anymore." I cut him off, not wanting to get into it. "Phil's gone and we don't have to be in each other's lives. But I do feel like I have to tell them about the letter."

"Why? You don't owe them anything." Miles grimaced.

"It's not about that. If they can give me some insight into what he might've meant—"

"Would they do that, though?" James asked.

"Not for me, no. But if it means finding out the truth about what happened to him—*if* something did—I have to believe they would try. The Tanners are powerful. They have resources and contacts. If anyone can pull strings, it's them."

"What exactly are you hoping to find?" Eric slowly peeled the paper from his beer bottle.

"I... I don't know, exactly. Maybe he had enemies at work. A client who was mad at him. Something. If they can tell me that, maybe it'll be enough to make the police reopen the case."

"You want the case reopened? Why?" James's expression was twisted with frustration, and I could tell he was trying to restrain himself.

"Because I think Phil's letter points to the fact that something happened to him or maybe something was going to happen to him. He'd been acting weird on the days leading up to the wedding. I just think maybe there's something I don't know. And, if he was in danger, maybe I'm in danger too. Whatever—*whomever*—he was trying to protect me from, maybe they're still out there. I have to know the truth, and this is the only way to do it."

"What if they don't know anything? Besides, it's been a year since... It's been a year. If you were in danger, don't you think you'd know about it by now? It really seems like you're reading too much into this letter." James looked like he wanted to say more, but instead, he lowered his chin, waiting for me to respond.

"What do you mean he'd been acting weird?" Eric asked, drawing my attention to him.

"Oh, um." I blinked to clear my head. "He'd been... standoffish. We had a fight a few days before." I cast a guilty look at James but didn't bother to explain further. "We nearly called the whole thing off."

"Holy shit..." Eric ran a hand over his chin, adjusting in his seat. "I had no idea. He never mentioned it."

"We worked it out, but he still seemed...off, I guess. Whenever I'd ask about it, he told me it was just pre-wedding jitters. Now, I'm wondering if there was more to it."

"So, you're sure about this? There's no changing your mind?"

I nodded slowly. "I want to talk to them. I have to."

Eric tipped his beer back, gulping it down and swiping the back of his hand across his forehead. "I'll do whatever I can to help you, Blondie. You know that. But..." He sighed. "Just... Just know that you might not like what you find."

Before I could ask him to elaborate, he stood, the chair scooting loudly under him before he moved toward the house, leaving me to bask in shadows and questions.

CHAPTER ELEVEN

WEDDING DAY

"Eric just got here." I heard the words before I realized James had entered the room. I spun around in my chair, placing my phone down.

"Dilma told me." I stood, smoothing my hands over my dress. James's eyes widened and he drew in an audible breath. His shoulders straightened, a red blush creeping up his neck.

"You look... Wow. You look beautiful, Colbie."

I looked down, pinpricks of embarrassment shooting through me. "You're not going to tease me about wearing too much eyeliner or how this side of my head didn't curl as well as that side?"

"Not today. I'll, uh, I'll take the day off." His smile was sad, his gaze raking over me. He opened and closed his mouth, looking away.

"Well, thank you for that. You, um, you look great too. You should wear a tux more often."

He chuckled. "I think I'll stick to my scrubs, thanks."

"You're telling me. I'll be glad to get out of this dress." I tugged at the ball gown skirt awkwardly.

At my words, it was as if something snapped. He stepped toward me, his gaze trancelike. There was no laughter in his expression, no room for jokes in the space he closed between us. He lifted his hand and, for a second, I thought he was going to cup my cheek. I held my breath, not sure what was happening. Why was he looking at me that way? I'd seen that look before, but never in his eyes. Never while looking at me. Moments before his skin connected with mine, I realized I'd misread the situation. The look was gone. I puffed out a breath of air as his hand landed on my shoulder. He cleared his throat. "You look just as good in your scrubs."

"Well, thank you. So do you."

He stepped back, nodding slowly. "Are you... Are you ready?"

"Just about." I checked the clock on the wall. "Is it filling up out there?"

"Yeah. A full house."

"Jerry's here."

"Did you expect him not to be?" He furrowed his brow.

"I didn't have any expectations."

He smashed his lips to the side, appearing annoyed. "You're allowed to expect things from the people in your life, Colbie. I know you've lost so much and...and been hurt so often, but that doesn't mean you can't have standards for the people who are still here."

"I know that..." Why did he sound so angry? "What are you getting at?"

He turned away from me suddenly, pacing.

"I'm just so sick of you letting everyone treat you however they want to because you think you might lose them if you stand up for yourself. If you, for a damn minute, just let them see who you really are, the ones who are worth anything will still be around."

He was shaking. Why? Where was this coming from? "Is this about Jerry? Or Phil?"

He spun back around, stopping in his tracks.

"I heard the two of you fighting, by the way. In the hallway earlier. Want to tell me what that was about?"

"We weren't fighting. We were...having an animated discussion." He gave me a stubborn, defiant look.

"About what?"

He hesitated, and I wondered if he'd lie or refuse to tell me, like Phil had. Instead, he took a breath. "It started with me asking him about Eric."

"Okay." I waited for him to elaborate when he didn't immediately go on.

"He didn't seem to know or care where he was and that bothered me. I told him it was stressing you out, and he suggested *giving you a glass of wine.*"

James paused, letting the words carry the significance he obviously thought they deserved. I wouldn't lie and say the disregard in Phil's words didn't sting.

"As if you were just being dramatic. So, I asked him if he even cared about you at all because it sure as shit doesn't seem like it most days—"

91

"James—"

"Don't. I know you love him, Colbie. You've made that clear. I know you're willing to overlook a lot, but I have a right to know. He's marrying my best friend. I have a right to be protective, if you won't protect yourself."

"Protect myself from what, exactly?"

He pressed his lips together, an obvious internal struggle going on. "You're blind when it comes to him."

"I am not!"

"Colbie, never once have I known you to let anyone get away with as much as you let him get away with."

"You have no idea what you're talking about." I turned away from him, anger radiating through me.

"How many times has he missed dinner with you? How many parties have you not been invited to? How many times has he canceled plans last minute?"

"Work stuff. He works hard. His job requires a crazy amount of hours."

"And trips out of town."

"Yes."

"Trips that you are never invited to go along on."

"I have work. Besides, I knew all of this when we started dating."

"And you're just going to be okay with that forever?"

"I mean, eventually, things will calm down. Once he's made partner and—"

"Yeah, okay. If you believe that, you're not as smart as I've always thought."

"Where is all of this coming from, James? Why haven't you mentioned it before?"

"I have!" He was breathless and frustrated, but so was I. We could go toe to toe any time. "I've mentioned it countless times. Sure, I get it, he's charming. That's his job. He schmoozes you, Colbie. He doesn't take care of you. He knows all the right things to say when it comes down to it, but when is he ever there for you when you need him? When it actually counts." He paused, his chest rising and falling with heavy breaths.

"That's not fair."

"It's not? Who took you to the store when your car was in the shop? Not Phil. Who brought you soup that week you had the flu? Not Phil. Who helped you repaint your apartment before you moved out? Not Phil."

"So, what? You just stop being my best friend because I'll be married? I'm not allowed to ask you for things because I'm getting married now? Is that what you're saying?"

He pressed his lips together. "You know that's not what I'm saying. I never mind helping you, but he should *want* to. You shouldn't even have to ask. You're engaged. I should have to fight for your attention and, instead, you have to fight for his."

"You're not being fair."

"Aren't I?" He shook his head. This time, his tone was soft. Almost apologetic. I got the feeling he regretted even bringing it up. "Because if you can go through with this wedding and tell me it's everything you've ever dreamed of, fine. But...if you have any doubts, if you even think you might want something else...you're running out of time to say so. And I'm running out of time to ask you."

"I love him." I was crying then, unable to stop the tears that streamed down my cheeks.

"Does he love you?"

"How can you ask me that?"

"Why can't you answer?"

"Because it's a stupid question, you jerk. Of course, he loves me. He's *marrying* me, James. *He* asked *me* to marry him, if you remember. Not the other way around."

"What do you even see in the guy, Colbie? Is it...is it just because the dude looks like a walking J. Crew model? Or is it his job? His money—"

"You did not just ask me that!" I shouted, shoving a fist toward the ground with disdain. "Is that really what you think of me? That I'd marry someone for any of those reasons? Do you honestly believe I'm that shallow?"

"What is it, then? Because you've never been able to give me an answer."

"*Screw you.* I don't owe you anything, James. If this is how you feel, if you think I shouldn't marry him, why would you even agree to be my man of honor? Why are you even here? Are you just trying to ruin my wedding day?"

"What? No. Of course not. I—" He stepped forward, reaching for me, but I backed away. "I'm sorry. This has gotten so out of control. That's not my intention. I didn't plan to do this. Please, know I never... I never planned to... God, please don't cry." He tilted his head to the side, his eyes panic-stricken. "Please. I won't say another word about it if you promise me you're happy. That's all I want."

"I'm happy." I reached for tissues, dabbing my cheeks. "I'm the happiest I've ever been."

He swallowed, dragging his head down with a slow nod.

I was happy, wasn't I?

This morning, I would've sworn it was true. Why then, in that moment, did it all suddenly feel like a lie?

CHAPTER TWELVE

PRESENT DAY

Eric was in the shower by the time we made it inside. I desperately wanted to talk to him about what he'd said around the fire. About me finding out things I didn't like about Phil, but I got the feeling he was trying to avoid exactly that.

It was my night to room with Miles, so I rolled my bag into his room and sank onto the spare bed.

Paying me no attention, he pulled his shirt over his head and I admired the ink on his skin. Like a tapestry, the tattoos ran up his sides, across his chest, and down his arms.

He grinned when he noticed me staring. "Everything okay?"

"Mm-hmm." I looked away, hoisting the suitcase onto the bed. It was ridiculous how attractive he was, and he knew it.

"Still thinking about what I said earlier?"

I nodded. "I can't stop."

"Do you know your answer?"

His stare burned into me, but I didn't dare look up. Heat crept up my neck. "Do I love him, you mean?"

"That's exactly what I mean."

I cut a sideways glance at him. "I don't know, Miles. It's all so complicated."

"I think you do know. You have to. And maybe you're afraid—whether it would hurt yourself or him, I don't know. But you know how you feel."

I tucked in my upper lip.

"My bed's under the fan." The conversation shifted so quickly, I tugged my head back with shock.

"What?"

When I looked over, he was pointing up. "The vent's right above it and it throws the air really well, so this room gets cold. I figured you'd be better off in that one. Unless you get hot when you sleep and then we can switch beds, but I didn't want you to get too cold."

"This is fine." I could barely bring myself to look at him, the constant pressure of his question in my head.

Do you love him?

Miles challenged me in ways the others didn't. While Eric and James sometimes treated me with kid gloves, Miles pushed me to speak up for myself, to be bolder.

Sometimes, I appreciated it.

Sometimes, I just wished he'd shut up.

"There are extra blankets in the top of the closet if you get too cold."

"Thanks." I pulled my pajamas from the suitcase and clutched them at my chest. "Um...I should change."

"Right." He ran a hand through his hair, pulling the door open. "Eric's still in the shower. I'll step out here. Just let me know when you're done."

With him out of the room, I quickly stripped out of my clothes and replaced them with my pajamas.

"Done."

With my toiletry bag in hand, I made my way across the room and sat down in front of the small vanity. My freckles were more prominent from my time in the sun, and my hair was wild and frizzy around my hairline thanks to the hours spent in the water.

In the mirror, I saw the door open again, and Miles reappeared. He met my eyes as he shut the door, holding my gaze for longer than necessary.

When he reached his bed, he cleared his throat. "I sleep in my boxers."

"Do you want me to—" Before I could finish the question, he'd already pulled his pants down with one swift motion, revealing a pair of bright-red boxer briefs. I looked away in an instant.

"I warned you." He pulled back the covers and slipped into his bed, rolling over. I unzipped my bag, pulling out my acne medication and moisturizer and applying them generously, my skin burning from the humiliation over what had just happened.

It wasn't that Miles was trying to make me uncomfortable. We'd spent the better part of a year together. At this point, we knew quite a lot about each other. But over that time, I'd come to realize he just didn't care about things that made most people uncomfortable.

He was here for all of the awkward conversations and the blunt remarks. There was no filter on him, no room for shame or embarrassment, and no place for awkwardness.

Miles was just Miles. Plain and simple, and exactly how he presented himself to you.

It was both refreshing and intimidating.

Moments later, I heard the shower shut off and the bathroom door open.

"I should go brush my teeth." I wasn't sure why I was announcing it. Truthfully, I was hoping to catch Eric in the hall, but I didn't want Miles to see that.

"That's a good idea."

He smirked at me from where he lay, his eyes closed as I made my way into the hall, bag still in hand. The bathroom light was off, his bedroom door shut, and I cursed my timing as I flipped the light back on. The bathroom was still steamy from Eric's shower, the mirror covered in fog. I ran a hand over the glass and wet my toothbrush.

I felt the cool air from the hallway before I saw the door opening again. James stood there, a look of uncertainty on his face, toothbrush in hand. He smiled, and I sidestepped, giving him space next to me.

We brushed in awkward silence. Miles's question swam through my head, along with the fight James and I had on my wedding day. So much had happened that day, I hadn't thought about it in a year, but now, it was all I could think about.

When I returned to the room, I put my bag and suitcase on the floor, tucked them at the end of the bed, and slipped under the covers.

The room was pitch black, just the whirring of the fan to interrupt the silence. I was grateful I could no longer see him. That he could no longer see me worrying.

He seemed to enjoy it.

"You're quiet tonight."

"Just...a lot on my mind."

"Penny for your thoughts?"

"I don't want to bore you."

"You could never bore me." I couldn't tell if he was being sarcastic.

"You know, if you'd told me a year ago that we'd be spending a weekend together, I never would've believed it."

The bed springs squeaked from across the room. He was trying to get comfortable, most likely.

"Yeah? Why not?"

"Well, a year ago, you were a stranger, first of all."

He chuckled under his breath. "Yeah, I was."

"I've never asked you, but...what made you... What made you come to my house that day? After Phil died?"

He didn't answer right away.

"Is that okay to ask?"

"You can ask me anything you want, Colbie." His words sent goose bumps over my arms. "You know that." I pulled the blanket up farther toward my shoulders. "I saw his obituary online, and... I don't know. It felt wrong not coming to at least tell you how sorry I was, but it also felt weird coming to a funeral when I didn't really know you. I still had your address from the wedding contract, so I thought it would be less awkward if I dropped by when you weren't surrounded by people." He sighed. "And, to be honest, I just wanted to be sure you were okay. I couldn't even imagine what you must've been feeling. So, I grabbed some flowers and headed over, against my better judgment."

"Why against your better judgment?"

He chuckled dryly. "Oh, hell, for all the reasons. I didn't know if you'd even remember me, I didn't know if I was overstepping, I wasn't sure if you'd be open to company. I've never really been good at that stuff."

"Well, for the record, it meant a lot to me."

"I know. You've said."

"I'm glad you know. And then you agreed to sing at the funeral, which in hindsight was probably a crazy request, given that it was the next day."

"I was happy to do it for you." *For you.* I hadn't missed the way he'd said that. Not for Phil. Never for Phil. He released a dramatic breath. "And now you're stuck with me."

"Surprise of my life."

"Mine too."

We were quiet for a while, both lost in thought for so long I thought he might've fallen asleep.

When he spoke again, his voice was softer. "Were you friends with Eric before that night? I know he was Phil's friend, but was he yours too?"

"We were...close, I think."

He snorted. "You think?"

"I mean, not like we are now, but we were together a lot because he was always with Phil. They were like brothers."

"Does that make it awkward for you now?"

"Not really. If anything, it's been good to be close to someone else who misses him. Eric doesn't really have anyone else either. Not a lot of family. Not a lot of friends." I wished I hadn't phrased it like that. "I'm making him sound pathetic. He's got plenty of friends, but none that knew Phil. So, we were kind of each other's person throughout all we went through. And, yeah, we've definitely gotten closer because of it."

"It's good that you had him. No one should go through a loss like that alone."

Something in his tone made me pause.

"Have... Have you lost someone?" Sometimes I felt like I hardly knew Miles. We spent so much time talking about me, about my pain and my loss and my life, there was very little time for talking about him.

"Yeah, a few people." He was adjusting in bed again. "It sucks, but it's life."

"I'm sorry, Miles."

"Don't be sorry, kiddo. Some good comes from it, if you look hard enough."

"Like you for me."

I could hear the smile in his voice. "Like me for you."

This time, the pause lasted even longer than before. When I spoke, my voice was soft. I didn't want to wake him if he'd dozed off. "Miles?"

To my surprise, his response was instant. "Yeah?"

"What do you think Eric meant earlier? About not liking what I find out about Phil?"

"If you give them long enough, everyone will disappoint you eventually."

His words shocked me, though I'd lived a large part of my life believing the same thing. "Not everyone."

"Everyone." There was no room for negotiation in his tone.

"Are you going to disappoint me?" My voice was soft, so quiet I didn't know if he'd hear.

"If I haven't already."

"You haven't."

"Give me time," he teased.

The air kicked on overhead and, just as he'd warned, the fan blew it quickly toward me. I shivered, my body covered in goose bumps. "Did you say there were more blankets in the closet?"

The bed creaked with his weight and, in seconds, I heard the closet door opening.

"I would've gotten it." I pressed my lips together, sitting up in bed.

The metallic *chiiiing* of the cord attached to the light bulb in the closet sounded as Miles pulled it, his silhouette suddenly in clear view. He pulled two fuzzy blankets down and brought them to me.

"I didn't think you were tall enough to reach."

Fair point. At exactly five feet tall, it would've been a stretch for me at best. His six-foot frame didn't share that struggle.

"Well, thank you."

He shook out the first blanket, leaning down to tuck me in as I lay back. "Do you need another?"

He was so close to me, I could feel his warmth, his hands on either side of me. "One's good."

He nodded, but he didn't move his hands. I could barely make out his expression in the dark, all shadows and darkness, but I was sure I could see a vague hint of a smile on his lips.

"I'm going to go back to my bed now."

"Good night."

He still wasn't moving, his weight planted next to me on the bed. He lifted his hands slowly, running them down the length of my arms and stopping at my wrists. "Good night."

Warmth spread throughout my chest, and it wasn't from the blanket. "You're not moving."

"Do you want me to?"

"I..." I couldn't find the words, didn't know the answer. Nothing about this made sense. Miles was attractive, no doubt, but I wasn't attracted *to* him. Was that why he'd asked about James? Did he have feelings for me too? "I don't want to complicate things." I managed to finally squeak out the words.

He'd made no further advances, waiting for my answer, and when I gave it, he pulled his hands back at once.

"I'm sorry." What was I apologizing for? Turning him down? Was that what I'd done? Or maybe for being so confused?

He shook his head, rubbing a playful hand over my

head—like a dog, or a small child. "Why would you be sorry?" He stood slowly, and moments later, he'd turned off the light in the closet and I heard his bed shift under his weight. "You finally admitted you actually know what you want. There's an opinion in there after all."

I lifted up on my elbows. "Wait, was that some sort of test?"

He laughed into his pillow. "Maybe."

"Not funny."

"Time to start trusting yourself, Colb." He shifted in the bed again, his voice muffled. "Now, go to sleep."

I tossed and turned, trying to find the elusive sleep I seemed to have to chase more often than not these days. After what must've been an hour, I heard Miles's steady breathing turn into soft snores.

I eased the covers off of my legs and stood. The floorboards creaked under me as I made my way across the room. I listened for his snoring to break or for him to ask where I was going, but it didn't happen.

He slept peacefully as I slipped out into the hall.

To my surprise, a dim light shone from under Eric's door.

Changing direction from the kitchen for a glass of water, I turned toward his room. When I reached it, I knocked cautiously, wondering if he'd fallen asleep with it on.

"Yeah?" His answer came immediately, a soft whisper.

I pushed the door open to see him sitting at his desk,

laptop open. His hair was unkempt from the shower, and he was dressed in sweats.

"Blondie? What are you doing up?" His brows crashed together. "Are you okay?"

"I'm fine, I just couldn't sleep."

His shoulders slumped. "Oh, well, in that case, join the club." He stood from his chair and moved across the room, sitting down on one bed and patting the space across from him on the other.

"I used to be able to fall asleep as soon as I hit the bed." I sighed. "The things I took for granted."

"It changed after he died?"

I nodded. Based on the haunted look in his eyes, I assumed he could relate.

"Listen, I'm sorry about earlier. I shouldn't have stormed off and said what I said."

"Why did you?" I pressed.

"To be honest, I don't know. Part of me is scared of what we'll find. Scared that we'll find something he didn't tell me about and... And what does that mean? In my head, he was my brother. I told him everything. He knew everything there was to know. But what if he didn't tell me everything back? Does that change who we were? I don't know if I'm ready to reckon with that."

"No matter what we find, Phil thought of you like a brother too, Eric. You know that. You were his best friend."

He looked away, a wary expression on his face. "I don't want you to get hurt either. If there's anything to find—"

"So you think there is?"

"I don't know." He kneaded his hands together.

"Did you really not know about our fight before the wedding?"

He shook his head. "No, honestly, I didn't. He told me you guys got into it over something stupid, but I didn't know it was that serious. I assumed it was like...him leaving dirty clothes out or something. Not enough to nearly call off the wedding."

I turned my head, unable to meet his eyes. I wanted to sound casual as I said what would come next, though it still felt anything but casual. It stung as badly now as the day James told me. "I thought he was cheating on me."

His shoulders stiffened. "Wait, what? Why would you think that?"

"Someone saw him out with another girl when I was out of town picking up my sister before the wedding."

"What girl?"

"I don't know. *A* girl. Short blonde hair." I held my hands near my chin, the way it had been described to me. "Tan. Pretty."

When I turned back to meet his eyes, I tried to decide if there was anything in them that would tell me whether it was true. Any sign of a confirmation. His eyes were empty. Void of all emotion.

"What did he tell you?"

"He said it was crazy. Nonsense. That he'd been working all weekend and hadn't left the house."

"Did you believe him?"

"I don't know, to be honest. I think so, yes. I mean,

with as much as he traveled, I'd always worried some, but he swore to me there was nothing going on. I wanted to trust him. Needed to. So, I told myself it had to have been a misunderstanding. But part of me..." I trailed off, unsure I could admit what I'd thought at the time.

"What?"

I squeezed my eyes shut. "Part of me knew it was easier." I was so ashamed to say the words out loud. "Our wedding was already planned and paid for. I didn't want to disappoint anyone. People had already started arriving in town. They'd already booked flights and hotels and... I don't know. I guess to call it off then would've felt like the worst thing in the world. It sounds so stupid when I say it out loud."

"I get it, though."

"I did love him, Eric. More than anything. And so, maybe it was just easier to convince myself I believed him, even if I wasn't totally sure. Do you think that was wrong?"

He stared at his hands, wringing them together as I'd often seen him do during intense negotiations with clients. "I don't know what's wrong or right anymore, honestly. I know he loved you. I do. And I know how devastated he would've been to lose you." He ran his teeth over his bottom lip. "I don't know anything about any girl. If he ever cheated on you, I swear, he didn't mention it to me."

I nodded, not entirely reassured. "Are those the kind of things you're worried we might find out? Maybe he got involved with a girl who was dangerous? Or who was married? Maybe it was something like that?"

"Maybe," he mumbled, his words a gut punch. I desperately needed to change the subject.

"Did you ever remember why you were late to the wedding, by the way?" I didn't say the next question out loud, but what I really wanted to know was whether he'd been obsessing over it as much as I was.

He ran a hand over his face. "I didn't. It's been such a blur of a year, and I was such a mess back then."

I nodded. "James and Phil fought about it. James was trying to find out where you were, but Phil wasn't worried. I overheard them arguing about it, and then James and I had a huge fight afterward." I was suddenly so tired, I was spilling everything on my mind before I'd planned to.

"That doesn't surprise me."

I cocked my head to the side. "What doesn't?"

"Well, it's not like it's the first time they fought."

"That's what I'm hearing." Apparently everyone knew this but me.

"You didn't know?"

I shook my head.

"They fought all the time, Colbie. I mean, not like physical fights, but Phil was always complaining about him, telling me things they'd said to each other or things James had done. He... I know James is your best friend, but Phil never liked him. I'm surprised you didn't know that. It was kind of hard to miss."

"I...had no idea. I mean, I knew they weren't *best*

friends," I admitted, "but I thought they got along alright."

"He always knew James had a thing for you. He trusted you, but that didn't mean he wasn't jealous—even if he was too proud to admit it." I must've had a strange look on my face, because Eric's expression shifted and he asked, "What?"

"Nothing. It's just... No one has ever said that before today. About James. And now, surprisingly, you're the second person to tell me he has feelings for me in a matter of twelve hours."

"Wait... You mean you didn't know?" He was looking at me as if I was the most naive person on the planet. Maybe I was.

"No. I... Well, looking back now, I guess, maybe there were signs. Moments, you know? But he's never said anything. Never tried anything. We were always just friends. He was always just...James."

"To be honest, I always thought maybe you had a thing for him too. Until I started spending time with the two of you together. From a distance, it looks different."

I nodded, a new idea crossing my mind. "Hey. Do you know if Phil and Miles knew each other before the wedding?"

"Miles?" His forehead wrinkled. "No, did they?"

"I don't know. It sort of seemed like it when they were introduced at the wedding."

"Did you ask them?"

"Yeah, but they both told me they didn't."

"And you don't believe them?"

"I didn't say I don't. It's just a feeling I get."

"Phil knew everyone." He chuckled nostalgically. "So, it wouldn't surprise me if they somehow knew each other. But why would Miles lie?"

"I don't know." I released a silent yawn.

"I should let you go to sleep. I'm beat." As he released a yawn of his own, he stood, moving toward the head of his bed. He didn't tell me I should leave, but I knew my welcome had been worn out. I had to go, even though there were a million more questions spinning in my head.

Why would Miles lie?

Would he lie?

Would Phil?

CHAPTER THIRTEEN

WEDDING DAY

They'd put me in a smaller room to wait for the ceremony to start. I could hear voices outside of the room—people laughing and carrying on while the music played in the background.

I checked the time on my phone. In just half an hour, Jerry would join me in the room, the music would shift, and then it would be time for him to escort me down the aisle.

I tried to convince myself the sweat on my brow was from the claustrophobia of the small, closet-like room and not my fears over my impending nuptials as I pressed myself up against the door.

Was I making a mistake?

Why had I let James get into my head?

Why didn't I trust him?

Why should I?

He'd been wrong about Phil's cheating, after all.

Indignation swelled in my chest. Why was James so

hell-bent on pushing us apart anyway?

As much as I tried to convince myself it was all going to be okay, I couldn't shake the worry that had settled in my gut as I was left alone with my thoughts. Amber and James were supposed to be with me, distracting me, keeping me calm, but Amber was off flirting with the guests and James...well, I wasn't even sure if he was still planning to be part of the wedding.

I swallowed down that thought.

Of course he was.

He might be angry with me. Hurt, even. But he wasn't cruel. James would be there for me like he'd promised. He always was.

I knew from the sounds of the music outside that Phil would still be waiting in his dressing room, probably toasting with Eric and Theo.

I didn't want to interrupt them—Dilma was likely to have a conniption if she caught me—but I had to see him. Just once more before we said our vows. I just needed to see his face and it would calm me down. Ease my nerves.

I waited for the music to switch, signaling that the guests would begin to take their seats. Once it had, the voices outside began to die down. When several minutes passed without me hearing anyone, I opened the door and peered out. Sure enough, the reception hall was empty except for the caterers and the band.

I listened for Dilma's voice, and once convinced I couldn't hear it, I darted across the hall, holding my dress up as I went to keep from tripping.

The groom's dressing room was two doors down in a

separate hallway from where I'd gotten ready. As I approached it, I could hear their laughter.

The sound of it soothed me enough that I was practically convinced I could turn back around.

But I didn't.

I knocked on the door softly, and Eric answered. As his gaze flicked over me, he whistled. "Hot damn, Blondie." Stepping back so the other two men in the room could see me, he shook his head appreciatively. "You sure you don't wanna switch grooms?"

"Back off, boys. She's all mine." Phil gave a cocky grin, crossing the room and holding an arm up between Eric and me. When he saw the expression on my face, his smile fell away. "Everything okay?"

"C-can I talk to you?"

Suddenly, I was on the verge of crying.

Again.

The room fell silent, all hints of laughter and playfulness dying away as Theo and Eric filed out of the room. Phil shut the door behind them, enveloping me in his arms.

"You shouldn't be here," he whispered as he kissed my lips hungrily. "Why are you crying, baby?" He stepped back, taking in the sight of me. "You're scaring me. You're not getting cold feet on me now, are you?"

"No. No. Nothing like that." I swiped my fingers under my eyes. "I'm sorry. I'm a mess today."

"That's understandable. I'm nervous too."

"But you think it's the right thing, don't you?"

"What are you talking about? Of course it's the right

thing." He led me to a chair, easing me into it, and sat down across from me. "Where is this coming from? What's going on in that pretty little head of yours?"

"I'm just scared, I think. And sad, but I don't understand why. I wish my mom could be here. And my dad. Jerry's here, but it's not the same. And James and I got in this big fight, and it's just... This isn't how it's supposed to go."

"Come here." He pulled me into him, allowing my face to rest on his shoulder. "I'm sorry. I would do anything to be able to have your parents here with us today. I know how much that would've meant to you. We have chairs for them up at the front though, right? I'm sorry today isn't everything you dreamed of—"

"It is. No, it really is. I'm sorry. You've been so amazing with helping me set this up. I shouldn't be complaining to you—"

"Complain to me, Colbie. That's what I'm here for. That's all I want. I'm glad you told me. I'm glad you're talking to me."

"It's the worst timing possible."

"It's our day. We set the timing."

"And I'm getting makeup all over your tux." I sat up, spying the pale stain on his shoulder. I attempted to scrub it away.

"I don't care about my tux, baby. I care about you." He pulled my hands down, kissing my knuckles, then my lips again. "Are you okay? Is there anything I can do?"

"Just hold me." I let him wrap his arms around me,

115

swallowing me up in a hug so warm I nearly forgot where we were. "This is going to be okay, isn't it?"

"Are you kidding? It's going to be amazing." He rested his cheek on my hair. "And some days, it won't be. Some days it will suck. But even on those days, I'm still going to love you. And you're still going to be stuck with me."

I giggled, my fears nearly gone. I sat back, rubbing my hair from my eyes. "I don't know what I ever did to deserve you."

"Just got lucky, I guess." His eyes shot playfully toward the ceiling.

I grinned halfheartedly. "I should get back. I just... I don't know. I needed this."

"Are you sure? We'll stay in here as long as you need. I'll book an extra week. I'll buy the place if you want."

I laughed. "Shut up."

He jutted his head toward the coffee table next to us, reaching forward for two of the three shot glasses. "Here. How about some liquid courage?"

I stared down into the clear liquid. It wasn't the smartest thing. I wanted to have a clear mind when we did this, but I'd never been able to tell Phil no.

I lifted the glass to my lips, tilting it back and swallowing without a hint of hesitation.

Don't let them see your fear.

That was the advice Phil had given me once, when he'd encouraged me to ask for more money at work, and the same applied now.

With the warm liquid still burning my throat, Phil grinned at me.

Always in command.

Always charming.

That was the man I loved.

"Now, let's go get married."

CHAPTER FOURTEEN

PRESENT DAY

The next morning, when I awoke, I was alone in the bedroom. I sat up, my body cold and stiff. As my feet hit the hardwood floor, I spied Miles's suitcase open on the bed.

His guitar case still sat in the corner.

Had he played it at all since we arrived?

I reached under the bed and pulled my toiletry bag out, making my way to the vanity to apply my acne medication and moisturizer. I took my vitamin and birth control pill and stared at my face. The tan that had been there last night looked faded in this light. My cheeks were flushed from sleep, my hair even messier than the night before. I pulled it down from its ponytail and retrieved my spray, dousing my curls and attempting to scrunch them back to life.

Once I'd given it all I had, I moved back across the room, stopping near Miles's bed as a pang of curiosity hit me.

It was wrong to snoop, but really, what harm could it do?

He'd left it open, after all, and I'd seen him in his underwear last night. What else could there possibly be?

I picked up a bottle of cologne he'd haphazardly thrown into the bag and popped off the lid. I placed it to my nose and inhaled. The scent was musky and wild— one I'd smelled a thousand times by now.

I placed the lid back on and turned my attention to a golden photo frame in the mesh netting of his suitcase. I checked over my shoulder to be sure I was still alone and then, with my heart pounding, I unzipped the compartment and reached for it.

I turned the frame over in my hand, studying the picture. It was Miles from several years ago—younger, shorter hair, innocent, though he was trying to look tough. He had his arm around the girl standing next to him, her waist-length blonde hair pulled forward over her shoulders, eyes nearly hidden behind the glare of her glasses.

"What are you doing?"

I jumped, nearly dropping the frame, as I turned to see Miles standing in the doorway, a towel wrapped around his waist, hair drenched from a recent shower.

"I was... I'm sorry... It was open and—"

He shut the door behind him. "You were snooping in my bag?"

"I'm so sorry, Miles. Honestly, I just walked past and, well, curiosity got the best of me. It's no excuse. I understand if you're mad at me and— Wait. Are you smiling?"

His rage-filled expression had softened, then it upturned into a smirk. "Chill, Colbie. I was joking. If I was worried about you going through it, I wouldn't have left it open."

I breathed a sigh of relief as he moved around me and tossed his dirty clothes into the suitcase.

"Who is this girl? In the picture with you. She's beautiful. I've never seen her before, and you haven't mentioned her. Is it an ex or a friend or... Obviously someone you've known a long time. And someone important enough to bring a photo with you everywhere you go. A real photo too, not on your phone..."

"Are you going to be quiet long enough to let me answer?" He laughed, digging through his clothes. "That's my little sister."

Something twinged deep in my gut. *What grown man walks around with a picture of his sister in his luggage? I don't even have pictures of my sister in my house.*

"She died."

Ice slid down my spine, the wind sucked from my lungs.

"Oh."

"Yeah."

"I'm... Gosh, I'm so sorry."

"Thanks." He pulled a shirt over his head, then held out his shorts, obviously prepared to put them on whether I was there or not. I turned away to give him some privacy, but didn't leave the room. Not yet. Not when I was on the verge of actually learning something about him.

"Can I ask what happened?"

"It was an accident. A few years ago." I heard the towel drop to the floor.

"That's terrible. I'm sorry."

"You said that already."

"Were the two of you very close?"

"Growing up, yeah. But as we got older, we drove each other crazy. She was still my sister."

"Of course. I... I know how it feels. I lost my parents when I was young, my dad when I was ten. He was in an accident too—a car accident. It was raining and...it was awful. And my mom got sick a few years later."

"And then you lost Phil." He was closer than I'd been expecting, and when I turned around, he was fully dressed and holding his towel in one hand. Suddenly, I understood the ever-present storm clouds in his eyes. They looked something like my own.

"And then I lost Phil."

"I'm sorry too," he said, a certain sadness in his eyes I knew only someone who'd experienced what I had could possess.

"Thank you."

"Why don't you ever talk about her? I talk about Phil so often. You should've told me..."

He shrugged one shoulder. "I'm telling you now." He picked up the photo frame, tucking it back in the mesh compartment, and closed the suitcase without another word.

CHAPTER FIFTEEN

WEDDING DAY

"What is taking so long? We should have started by now. Dilma said it would just be a few more minutes over two hours ago."

Standing next to the door, his forehead slick with sweat, Jerry shrugged. "I don't know, kiddo. Want me to go and find your sister? She'll know what's going on."

Amber had slipped out of the room over an hour ago, claiming she had to use the restroom. If I knew her, and I did, she was probably nose deep in whatever drama was delaying the ceremony.

Dilma mentioned something about a seating chart and an issue with the band, but placed a glass of champagne in my hand and assured me it was all handled.

I chewed my bottom lip. "I don't know. I'm trying not to panic." I picked up my phone from the bookshelf. "Phil hasn't texted me back."

"I'm sure it's fine." He was trying to hide worry of his own, but I saw through it.

I pressed my ear to the door, trying to get a sense of what was going on out there. Outside, I could hear the faint sounds of live music, though the band was only meant to play the reception.

What was going on?

Something was very wrong.

I could feel it in my gut.

I wished someone would tell me something.

"I'm going out." Jerry stepped back, appearing relieved as I swung the door open. A handful of guests were gathered in the reception area. Aunt Irene was there, fanning herself, her feet up in the chair next to her. In the distance, James was writing a letter for our wedding box.

My boss, Annie, waved to me, drawing my attention, her eyes wide.

"Oh, honey, you look beautiful!" She rushed my way, causing a few other guests to notice me too. It was a disaster. This wasn't how it was supposed to go.

She gathered me in for a quick hug, kissing both cheeks. The smell of cigarettes filled my nostrils. "I bet Phil is just ready to eat you up."

I blushed, glancing awkwardly at Jerry. "Um, Annie, what's going on? Have you heard why it still hasn't started?"

Her brows pinched together. "I was going to ask you the same thing. Your wedding planner just said there was going to be a slight delay and that they were serving ice water in here in case anyone needed to cool off."

She gestured toward the waiter who'd just rounded a

corner carrying a tray of drinks. "I just came in to get a drink before I went back outside to listen to the band play. They've got a cute little setup out there, and they're actually not bad. I must say, I'm not one bit bothered by the delay if it means I get to keep staring at them." She winked. "Any chance the singer is single?"

A laugh escaped her throat. "Sorry, ignore me. Anyway, spill. What's going on? Did you get cold feet? Need a little *alone* time with the groom before the wedding?" She winked again, and my face burned with embarrassment. Jerry stepped away, moving to talk to Aunt Irene. "I'll bet you crazy kids can't keep your hands off each other, but two hours?" She shielded one side of her face with her hand, as if she was telling me a secret. "*Wow*. What's his secret, hmm?"

"No, that's not it at all. I have no idea what's—"

A scream tore through the hall before I could finish my sentence, chills scrambling down my spine. "Help! Someone help!"

Vomit threatened to rise in my throat. The room spun, filled with terrified voices and hushed whispers.

Jerry was next to me once again, his hand on my arm. "What was that?"

Without thinking, I bolted toward the scream, racing out of the reception area and toward the hallway. A door swung open ahead of me—Phil's door—but it wasn't Phil standing there.

Dilma launched herself out of the room, phone in hand, her eyes wild with fear. She was trembling so much, she could hardly accomplish whatever she was trying to do.

I shoved past her into the room without pausing to ask what had happened. My blood chilled at the sight waiting for me.

Jerry was behind me. "What the hell?"

The floor was littered with glass from a broken champagne bottle, but I hardly noticed. Instead, my eyes fell to the floor, where my fiancé's body lay.

No. Please no.

I was at his side within seconds, a hand on his chest. I turned his head, trying to feel for a pulse. His chest was still, not rising or falling with steady breaths. There was no heartbeat under my fingertips.

I tried to make sense of it. To rationalize it. He'd fallen and he'd be getting up any moment.

It was fine.

This would all be okay.

It had to be.

It was Phil.

"Jesus." Jerry was next to me, though I hadn't even realized it until that moment. He put a hand over mine. "You should go, Colbie. You shouldn't be here."

My body tensed. "I'm not leaving him."

Suddenly snapping into action, I attempted to lift him. My knees dug into the glass on the carpet, and I screamed in pain, falling backward.

Jerry was dragging me away, everything happening in slow motion. I jerked free of his arms, sobs tearing through me.

No.

No.

No.

It wasn't possible.

It wasn't happening.

I reached Phil's body again and shoved his suit jacket out of the way, tearing his shirt open as I placed my cheek on his chest. It wasn't happening. It couldn't be.

I lifted up, shouting at anyone who would listen. "Someone help me! Please!" A tear fell onto his chest, and I placed my cheek on it again.

Was I supposed to do CPR? What was that song people used?

Was this a joke?

How was it possible?

My brain was fighting the reality, unable to accept what was happening.

"You can't die on me!" I screamed. I gripped his cheeks. "Baby, please... Wake up. Wake up, Phil. Come on. Come on. We have to get married, honey. Don't do this. You can't. Please. Please wake up." I pleaded with him as if he might've just casually stopped his heart to play a prank on me.

There was a commotion outside the room. I could hear Dilma trying to keep people back, but it wasn't working. The room had begun to fill with onlookers. Questions were flying around. At least five people were on their phone with 911 dispatchers.

"Shut up!" I shouted, trying to hear his heartbeat. The heart that was supposed to belong to me. "Shut up, all of you!" Jerry laid his jacket over the glass on the floor, pulling me onto it, but it was too late. My dress was torn, my knees, legs, and hands even worse.

Even as I stared at the blood, I couldn't feel it.

I couldn't feel anything.

One voice caught my attention.

"What's going— *Shit!*" That was James, who was at my side in a second, checking on me, and then Eric.

"*No. No. No.*" Eric was at my side, practically pushing me out of the way in an attempt to get to his friend. His brother. "What the fuck, man?"

I couldn't speak. Couldn't answer. Couldn't breathe. I crumpled on the floor, dragging my hands around in search of my phone.

Where did I leave it?

No.

It was still in the room.

"What are you looking for?" Dilma reappeared, looking more collected than she had moments ago.

"I need my phone!" I screamed at her, my voice wild and feral.

"Honey, the ambulance is on the way." Jerry's arms wrapped around me, holding me there on the floor in an attempt to calm me. To protect me from yet another loss no one could protect me from.

But no.

He wasn't gone.

He couldn't be.

Behind me, Eric was pacing and cursing, shouting at everyone in the room to leave or shut up or whatever else came to his mind, while James huffed and sighed with apparent attempts to resuscitate him.

I closed my eyes, wanting to shut it all out.

Wanting it all to stop.

A single sentence from James brought me back.

"I think he still has a pulse."

I opened my eyes, choking on sobs as hope spread through me. "He's still alive?"

"I think so." He had his fingers on Phil's wrist. "It's faint, but it's there."

"Fix him!" I shouted, slamming both hands into his chest. "Do something. Fix him, James! Please, God, do something! Save him. Bring him back to me. I can't lose him."

He shook his head, allowing me to slam my hands into his chest over and over again. When Jerry reached for me, he held his hands up to stop him. He'd take the punishment—take my wrath—if he thought it would make me feel better.

I collapsed onto my side, curling up as more sobs overcame me. "Why aren't you doing anything?" I begged.

"I'm doing all I can." His eyes were sad. Broken. Tears streamed down his cheeks. "He's not breathing, Colbie." He leaned forward, placing his mouth over Phil's as I lost my sense of reality again. "All I can do is give him oxygen until the ambulance gets here."

The room blurred.

I was going to be sick.

This wasn't happening again.

"What happened?" Jerry asked, attempting to pull me to him again, though it was no use. "Who was with him?"

"We were. But...he wasn't feeling well." Eric stopped pacing, his voice choked with sobs. "He said he was feeling light-headed and asked us to give him a minute. He'd had a few drinks and not much food. I just thought he needed to let the buzz pass. I had one of the caterers bring him some food and water." He chewed his thumbnail, his eyes locked on Phil's body as James puffed another breath into his mouth. "I... I thought it was just cold feet. Colbie, I'm so sorry." It was one of the only times I'd ever heard him call me by my name.

"I came back to check on him, to see if we could get things moving, and I found him like..." Dilma couldn't finish the sentence, breaking off into sobs of her own, her arms wrapped around herself. "I'm so sorry."

"You left him?" I pushed myself up from the floor, staring Eric down in disbelief. "How could you leave him?"

His own eyes swam with tears as he sank onto the couch, guilt riddling his broken expression. "Fuck, I'm sorry. I didn't know... How could I have known?" He shot a look at James. "*Aren't you a doctor? Isn't there something else you can do?*" His harsh tone was directed at James.

James was calm. "Like I said, I'm doing all I can. I'm not a human doctor. He has a pulse, but he isn't breathing... Until they get here, all I can do is keep giving him rescue breaths. Did they give you an ETA?"

"Fifteen minutes." Dilma checked her watch. "It's been ten."

Jerry rocked me back and forth, his hand stroking my hair.

"Shit." James lifted up on his knees over Phil's body.

"What? What is it?" I demanded, sitting up.

He locked his hands together, arms straight and pinned down on Phil's bare chest. "I lost his pulse. Fuck. *Get her out of here!*"

Jerry grabbed hold of me, both arms under mine. "Come on, honey. You shouldn't be here. Let's get you out of the room." He attempted to stand, attempted to get me to move.

"I can't leave him!" I sobbed, deadweight in his arms.

Jerry sank down again, the damage already done as James set to work on Phil's chest. Jerry did his best to turn me away from Phil's lifeless body as we waited, but the sounds were almost worse than the visual.

Another group of people appeared in the doorway, and Dilma shooed them away, slamming the door and barricading herself in front of it. Outside, people were crying and shouting instructions at James. Asking what happened. What they could do.

No one could do anything but wait.

So, that's what we did.

But all the waiting in the world wouldn't have mattered.

He was gone, and he was never coming back.

CHAPTER SIXTEEN

PRESENT DAY

"You're getting burned." Miles studied my shoulders as he moved past me in the pool, the volleyball in his hand.

"Whatever. You just want me to get out so you guys will actually win."

"'Cause they can't win fair and square." Eric threw an arm around my shoulder, grinning proudly.

"Aren't you down by four points right now?" Miles grinned, moving back to take his place next to James, who winked at me.

"Only because you cheated with that last one." Eric released me, moving back into position.

"Yeah, you keep thinking that."

"The line is here." Eric pointed to the filter. "We agreed."

"He didn't go over the line." James was playfully defensive.

"He one-hundred-percent did."

"Oh, don't be a sore loser." Miles tossed the ball into the air and caught it.

"Whatever, next time it's out, there are no redos." I narrowed my gaze at him.

"Don't worry about that. I'm all warmed up now. Ready to kick some butt." This time, when Miles tossed the ball into the air, he spiked it in my direction. I leaped into the air and smacked it back.

"Attagirl!" Eric beamed, knocking the ball back to them when James hit it our way.

I moved as the ball spun toward me in the air, placing myself under it and jumping to spike it back their way.

"Got it!" Miles moved for it at the same time as James, but they both hesitated, then reached, their fingers seconds too late as it splashed into the water.

"*Yes!*" Eric scooped me up, spinning us around in circles with a triumphant cry. "Hell yes!"

"Is it time to switch teams yet?" James groaned.

"You just want my star player." Eric placed me down. "She's all mine."

"Star player's a bit of a stretch. She got lucky." Miles pursed his lips, his competitive side on full display.

I stuck my tongue out at him. "You weren't saying that last time when I was on your team."

"It's different in the water." He grabbed the ball, tucking it under his arm and against his waist.

"Excuses, excuses." I wrung out my hair, my wrist brushing my shoulder and sending a pang of pain across my skin. I winced and glanced down at the sunburn Miles had warned me about.

"Where are you going? You aren't getting away that easily," Miles called, chasing me as I moved through the pool on my way toward the steps. "We've still gotta make our comeback."

"I'm going to reapply sunscreen." I waved him off. "I'll be right back. Wait for me." I climbed out of the pool. "Does anyone need anything while I'm inside?"

All three men shook their heads, watching as I made my way across the deck and wrapped a towel around myself, drying my shoulders before heading for the house.

Inside, the cool air was painful to my warm skin, spreading goose bumps across my body. Once dry, I reapplied the sunscreen to my shoulders and face, and I grabbed a bottle of water from the fridge. I tapped my phone screen before exiting and froze at the sight of the notification on my screen.

Four missed calls.

Crap.

I placed the bottle down and dried my hands even more, unlocking my screen.

My stomach flipped when I saw her name.

Amber.

Why on earth would my sister be calling me?

Just as I thought it, the screen lit up again.

"Hello?"

"Well, thank God I'm not dead on the side of the road somewhere."

The joke was in poor taste, especially this weekend, but I let it go.

"I'm sorry. I was out in the pool. Did you need something?" I thought immediately of Jerry and his cold. Had he gotten worse? Why would he call her first? "Is everything okay?"

"No, everything is *not* okay." She cursed under her breath. "People don't know how to drive in this stupid town."

I released a sigh of relief. "Everything *else* okay?"

"Ty and I got into a fight last night."

"Ty?" I couldn't keep up with the men she dated.

"The barista. Remember? I told you about him." I was silent, so she went on. "Anyway, I couldn't stay there. I needed to get out of town before he tried to come over. I took the next full week off, and I'm on my way to see you. Send me the address of your Airbnb."

"What?" Coldness swept through me. "I thought you were too busy to even check on Jerry this weekend, and now you can just take a week off?"

"I had to, Colbie. I couldn't take it anymore."

"No." It was the only word I could muster.

"No?" She scoffed. "Ha ha. Very funny."

"No, I mean, I'd love to see you, but we're only allowed to have four people here."

"It's fine. I can crash on the couch or wherever. I'm not picky."

"Why don't you stay with Jerry for the night? I'll be back home tomorrow and he could use the company."

"Because Jerry's sick, and I can't afford to catch it."

"Well, I don't know what you want me to say, Amber. I told the owner of the house there would only be four of us." I was more frustrated than I should've been, and I instantly regretted it.

"You're only staying there for one more night, aren't you? What's the big deal? Are you seriously going to refuse to let me come over? I have nowhere to go."

Frustrated again, I bit back the multitude of answers I wanted to give: *Not my problem. There are hotels. You should've given me a heads-up. Stop being so selfish. This is my weekend to grieve my loss and not everything's about you.*

Instead, I sighed, pinching the bridge of my nose, and said, "Fine. It's fine. We'll work it out somehow. I'll text you the address."

She squealed, blowing me a kiss through the phone. "You're the best, sis. See you soon."

BACK OUTSIDE, I walked with a slower pace, bubbles of anger and frustration filling my belly.

"About time," Eric said.

"We thought you fell in." Miles chuckled to himself.

"What's wrong?" It was James that caught and understood the worry in my expression.

I sank down onto the lounge chair next to the pool, flopping my hands into my lap. "Amber's on her way."

"What?"

"Why?"

"When?" came the three hurried responses.

"In a few hours. She's on her way from Tuscaloosa.

She got in a fight with her boyfriend and needs some time to cool off."

James shook his head. "She knows what this weekend meant to you."

"Amber has never cared what anything means to anyone."

"So tell her not to come." Miles sounded defensive. "You don't owe her anything."

"It's her sister." Eric sounded sympathetic.

"Stand up to her, Colbie. You don't need this right now. Not this weekend." Miles had moved toward the edge of the pool. His tone was firm.

"I can't. Eric's right. She's my sister, and she needs me. No matter what I have going on."

When I looked up, they each had apprehensive looks on their faces. What would this mean for our final night? What would it do to the atmosphere? It was so rare I got to spend uninterrupted time with my three closest friends, and I'd wasted so much of it already.

Amber's presence would change everything.

It always did.

"It'll be fine." That was James, trying to offer reassurance, though I felt none. "It's just one night."

"Is this what you want?" Miles's gaze and tone were pointed.

I forced a smile with a long inhale. "It'll be fine. We're all going home in the morning anyway, and today's half over."

With that, Miles tossed the ball across the pool and Eric caught it. "If you say so. One final game, then?"

· · ·

Two hours later, Amber's red Mazda pulled into the driveway, her horn beeping twice as she slowed it to a stop. We were all out of the pool by then, wrapped up in towels and sitting around the firepit.

Amber stepped from her car, pushing her sunglasses up over her hair. She waved with a hand over her head, bracelets jingling around her wrists.

"Yoo-hoo! Party's here!" She retrieved a paper bag from the back seat of her car. "Don't worry. I didn't come empty-handed." Her heels clicked across the driveway, then across the deck, and she came to a stop in front of us. "Well, Jesus, no one get up or anything."

I stood, wrapping one arm around her for a quick hug. "Hey."

"Hey." She heaved the bag down onto the small table next to James. "Looks like y'all need me worse than I thought." She shoved her fist into her hip. "What kind of a party is this?"

"It's not exactly a party," Miles grumbled.

"Well, I can see that." She seemed to take in the sight of him for the first time, a ravenous look filling her eyes. "I don't think we've met."

"Oh, we have." He didn't bother looking at her, moving forward instead to adjust a log on the fire.

"Amber, this is Miles and Eric." I gestured toward them both. "You guys met at Christmas last year."

"Oh, of course. That's right. Pleasure to see you both again." Her Southern accent was on full display. "James, good to see you too."

"Hey, Amber."

She glanced around, searching for a chair and claiming one next to James before reaching into the bag and pulling out a bottle of tequila. "Have you guys already started drinking?"

"It's two in the afternoon," Miles deadpanned.

Without missing a beat, Amber twisted the lid off the bottle. "It's a holiday weekend. Those rules don't count."

"So, what happened with Ted?"

"Ty," she corrected me. "And I caught him making plans to hang out with some girl he used to date."

"Were they going out on a date?"

She snorted, looking to James in hopes that he'd join her in the joke that wasn't so obvious to me. "A *date?* How long's it been since you were dating, sis?"

"What?"

She retrieved a stack of plastic shot glasses from the bag and filled one. "No one *dates* anymore. But they were planning to hang out, so I bounced. We weren't together, but we were exclusive." She tipped the shot back, swallowing it down as if it were water. "Not anymore, sucka."

"Maybe they were just friends," I offered. "Did you ask him?"

"They were exes. That's all I need to know. They can call me a lot of things, but they'll never call me stupid." She winked at James, who was visibly uncomfortable, and poured shots for us all. "Come on, guys, drink up. Last night here!"

She pushed our shots toward us. Eric reached for his first, then James, who seemed relieved to have something to do.

"James..." I shook my head. He knew I didn't like it when he drank more than a beer or two, after a particularly bad experience in high school when his blood sugar had dropped dangerously low.

"I'm good." He already knew what I was going to say. "I'll be good. I promise."

I stared at my shot. "I'm not really in the mood, Amber. And I haven't eaten."

"Oh, come on, Mother Teresa. It's one shot." She pushed it closer to me. "Lighten up. I'm not asking you to do a line of coke."

"She said no." Miles pushed his shot away too.

"Ooh, handsome and tough, hmm? Are you two a thing?" She wagged a finger between us.

"*No.*" I was too quick to answer, my face flushing with heat, my entire body filling with regret. Why had I agreed to let her come again? "I should get the grill started."

"Let's order in tonight." James leaned forward, placing his empty shot glass on the table. "We came here with plans to relax. Maybe Amber's right. Maybe we should take the final night to do that. All of us."

Amber squealed with delight. "Smart man. I always knew I liked him."

"We have to get up early to check out," I warned.

"I'll help you cook, if you want." Miles was studying me, a wary look on his face.

"James is right." Eric rubbed his hands over the arms of his chair. "We should relax. I'm not saying get plastered, but it's our last night. Have a drink. Let's order some food. Relax. What could it hurt?"

I sighed, clearly outnumbered. Amber had a way of doing that—getting everyone on her side. She'd even had Phil siding with her during disagreements before.

"Fine. I'm obviously outnumbered. But you're buying." I wagged a finger at Amber.

"Done." She clapped her hands together. "What'll it be?" She poured the drinks while we decided on our order, and I settled back into my chair.

The night would be what it would be, and there was nothing I could do to make it any more comfortable.

I reached for my shot glass, lifting it to my lips.

Might as well enjoy it.

CHAPTER SEVENTEEN

"I can't believe you don't remember that." Amber swatted James's chest, moving closer to him in the egg chair. Her cheeks were pink from the liquor in her system, her hair—straight and perfect where mine had always been frizzy in the slightest heat—pulled down from the bun she'd been wearing earlier.

James grinned at her, taking a sip from the cup in his hand. The drinks were getting stronger the later we made it into the night.

"I really don't." He was laughing along, no longer bothered by her presence. "Are you sure it was me?"

"I'm positive." She poked her finger in his chest then. "I wouldn't forget that, James Baker. You broke my heart. In fact, I demanded Colbie remove all the pictures of you from our house for, like...a month."

James looked at me, his eyes wide. "It's true." I shrugged one shoulder. "Though, it was more like three days. And you ended up going with Peter Hawthorne, who, if I remember correctly, you dated for, like, six months afterward."

"Well, I've always been resourceful if nothing else." She grinned shamelessly. "But, if *I* remember correctly, you told me you didn't want to go with someone who was two years younger than you, and then you ended up dating Ashley Gellar—who was in my grade—the next year."

James took another drink, his brows drawn down, then, as if suddenly realizing something, he pulled the bottle from his lips. "Holy shit. I do remember that, actually. I'd forgotten it was you." He cut a glance to me. "I can't believe you didn't tell me she was so upset."

"Would it have mattered?"

He looked at her then, though he was answering me. "I thought she was only asking because she didn't have anyone else to go with. I didn't want to be anyone's default." She leaned in closer to him and something flipped in my stomach. Ice-cold dread. "If I'd known you were really upset, I would've gone with you."

"I just figured you thought you were too old and too cool for me." She batted her eyelashes. "It was fine anyway. I was used to getting my heart broken by you at that point." She was joking, but I knew the truth of her words. I'd watched my sister pine over my best friend her whole life.

"What?" He straightened, stealing a glance from me and back to her.

"Oh, please. You weren't blind." She gave him an accusing stare.

"I had no idea." I wasn't sure if he was being honest, though I had no true reason to doubt him. It wasn't as if it would've mattered in the long run. James never would've gone for someone like Amber.

"Well, I don't know if that makes me feel better or worse." She laughed, moving to take a drink and pausing, eyeing her cup. "I need a refill." She slid forward in the chair, reaching for the tequila and mixing it with some of the Sprite we'd brought out.

When she slid back into her spot, she was closer to James, their bodies connecting at every point. He wouldn't catch my eye, so I had no idea what he was thinking.

My face was hot—from the alcohol or the situation, I couldn't tell—and I suddenly felt the urge to move or change the subject. I glanced up at the sky. "We should probably turn in for the night, don't you think? It's getting late and we have an early morning."

"Turn in?" Amber stiffened. "Already?" She checked the fitness tracker on her wrist. "It's not even midnight. The night is still young, sister dear. Let's..." Her eyes brightened. "Oh, let's play a game."

Eric and Miles, who'd been relatively quiet for most of the evening, adjusted in their seats.

"A game?" Eric winced.

"I'm not much on Monopoly." Miles ran a hand through his hair. "Colbie's right. It's late."

"Come on. One game." She held up a finger. "And I wasn't suggesting a board game."

"What'd you have in mind?" James asked.

I could see the mischievous glint in her eyes, and it worried me. "Amber, come on—"

"Truth or Dare." Her grin was wild and charming, as always.

"We are *not* playing Truth or Dare." I locked my jaw. What was wrong with her? She was twenty-six years old, not thirteen.

"Well, what's your suggestion, then?" she challenged, a single brow raised. "Party pooper."

"I don't want to play anything. It's late."

"Oh my god, you're such an old woman." She groaned. "It's not late. James wants to play... Don't you?" She eyed him expectantly, her every hope hanging on her words. My sister had never been subtle, never been one for keeping her mouth shut. She took after my mom in that way, while I remained the silent one like my dad.

Some days, I really hated that.

"I mean, I don't know..." He studied me, then looked back at her. "I can play, I guess."

I sighed.

"You don't have to play, Colbie." Miles was staring at me from across the firepit and, for just a moment, I worried he was just as annoyed with me as Amber was. "I'll go inside with you if you don't want to be alone."

"I'm fine. But...thank you." I needed to stay out there, to make sure Amber didn't cause trouble. If I left her alone with the boys—*my* boys—I was terrified to think of what would happen.

A sudden vision of clothing strewn about and bare

bodies molding together filled my mind, and I shoved it away.

These were my boys. My best friends. I needed them more than even they knew, and I couldn't let her take them from me. Couldn't let them see that she was the more fun sister. Couldn't give her the chance to start drama. Our balance was delicate and Amber was a train wreck that would threaten it all. I couldn't leave her alone with them.

"Alright, so we're all in?"

I leaned forward, filling and taking another shot, before rubbing my hands together. "Whatever."

"I'll go first," Amber cried, surprising no one. She placed her drink down and narrowed her gaze at me. "Sister, truth or dare?"

I answered without hesitation. "Truth." No way in hell I'd take a dare from her when she'd no doubt have me stripping or making out with someone in seconds. Those were the only dares I'd ever seen my sister dole out.

Her mouth pulled to one side in a twisted grin, and she wiggled her fingers together in front of her chin. "Alright, spill. How many of these guys have you had sex with?"

My jaw dropped open, heat shooting up my neck and into my cheeks. Miles chuckled, head down; Eric cleared his throat, adjusting his pants and leaning forward as if the game had just gotten interesting; and James stared at her, then me, watching carefully.

"None of them." I spoke through gritted teeth. How dare she come in and mess everything up? Already this weekend, I felt as if I were losing my handle on so much. Our usually pressure-free relationships had grown so complicated, and now, as if she could read the atmosphere, she had her thumb on our pressure points.

I couldn't lose them, but already, I could feel them slipping from my grasp.

I would be alone again if Amber had anything to say about it. If I didn't give them a reason to stay. If I couldn't make up my mind—though it was currently muddled with anger and grief.

"None?" She didn't believe me.

"No. None. They're my friends. Not everyone has the desire to sleep with every single person they meet."

"What's that supposed to mean?" She jerked her head back.

I waved her off, turning away. "Let's just move on. It's my turn. Eric, truth or dare."

"Um..." Eric was clearly still trying to catch up from everything that was happening. He shook his head rapidly. "D-dare. I guess."

"Okay, um..." I thought quickly. "Go through your phone and send a selfie to the last person you texted. No explanation."

He narrowed his gaze at me and pulled out his phone. "No. I can't do that. It's my client... Can I swap and choose truth?"

"No takesies backsies!" Amber taunted, giggling.

He groaned, casting a tauntingly annoyed look my way, but held out his phone and snapped a quick picture anyway, tapping the screen. "There. Done. If I lose this sale because of you, Blondie, I swear..." He wagged a finger at me, but he was smiling. His eyes were soft, his gaze sleepy from the alcohol in his system.

"Hey, don't blame me. I wanted to go to bed." I threw my hands up in proclaimed innocence. My body was warm from the fire and the alcohol and the adrenaline of the game, and I scooted farther forward, waiting for him to take a turn.

"Um... Let's see. Miles, I guess. Truth or dare?"

Miles waved him off. "Nah, man. I'm not playing."

"What? You have to play." Amber bounced up and down in her seat, her legs tucked up under her while she smacked her thighs with her hands. "If you're out here, you have to play."

"He doesn't have to..." I offered, feeling guilty as I saw the hesitant look in his eyes.

"If I have to, he has to!" Eric chuckled, his alcohol beginning to get the best of him. "Come on, man. You chicken?"

Miles rolled his eyes, as if he'd rather be anywhere else, doing anything but this. I half expected him to tell us all off, call us ridiculous, and go to bed. He was never the type to go along with something if he didn't want to. So why was he staying? For me?

He scratched his forehead with his thumb. "Whatever. Truth."

Eric chuckled. "Baby."

"Fuck you. Are you going to ask or not?"

"Alright, actually, there is a burning question I've

147

been meaning to ask you..." He tapped his chin with one finger.

I held my breath.

"How about... Who was the last person you searched on Instagram?"

The group released a collective sigh.

"What?" Miles stared at him.

"Come on. Show us... Who're you looking up? Your little band's competition? Celebrity crush? Old flame?"

Miles shook his head. "I have no idea. Probably my buddies. I'm not on there much."

"Show us."

"What? Hell no. I didn't pick dare." Miles's lips were tight. "Truth is an answer. Not an action."

"And you just said you don't know the truth. You're not giving us an answer, so you're going to have to put some *action* into looking it up."

From the way Miles was staring at Eric, I expected him to launch forward and punch him in the jaw at any moment.

"I'll bet it's an ex," Amber said.

Miles flashed a glance at me, then pulled his phone from his pocket. "Whatever. Like I said, I'm not on here much." He opened his phone and Eric moved to stand next to him.

"Looks like it was... Oh. Shit." Eric looked up at me, then back down.

"Don't." Miles warned. "Let's just end the game."

Before anything could be said, Amber jumped from

her chair and swiped the phone, holding it high above her head and reading aloud.

"Phillip…Tan*ner*." The last part of his name came out slower, as it connected for her.

The air was sucked from the space.

Every eye around the fire went to me.

Miles stood, reaching for his phone. "You didn't have to do that." Amber handed it to him, looking guilty.

"Why were you looking Phil up?" I asked softly, not sure I wanted to know the answer.

He wouldn't look at me, too busy closing the app and putting his phone away. "I think it was before we came here. I was probably looking for you and accidentally clicked his old account. I'm sorry."

"Did you know?" I asked Eric, the old familiar ache in my chest once more.

"I had no idea. Honestly. I'm sorry, Blondie. I wasn't trying to… We were having fun. I've seen other people do that as a Truth or Dare question, and it's usually embarrassing. I… I never thought… I didn't mean to bring it up."

It meaning him.

It meaning my heartbreak.

It meaning everything I'd lost.

I sank back in my chair, no longer in the mood to play the game. No longer in the mood to be around these people.

How could we play when Phil was dead?

When Phil would never get to live through a night like this?

When Phil's death might not have been accidental after all?

"Your turn." Amber took her seat next to James again, though the atmosphere had changed significantly. I hardly noticed as she rested her hand on his thigh.

"James," Miles grunted, not bothering to ask the implied question.

"Dare." James's voice was soft. Apologetic. The tension in the air was so thick, I could hardly catch my breath.

"Kiss her."

My head shot up at the words, half expecting him to be looking at me. Instead, I found Miles's eyes locked on Amber's, his jaw tight.

"What?" James and I asked at the same time.

"You heard me. Kiss her."

Amber turned to look at James, her smile so wide I was sure her cheeks must be burning.

He cut a glance at me, his mouth dropped open with an unspoken question. "Colbie, I..."

I shook my head, trying to play it off cooler than I felt. "It's just a stupid dare." Even as I said the words, my core fought against the lie. Why wasn't I stopping him? Why wasn't I telling him how badly this would hurt me? Better question: why didn't he know?

He looked from me to her and back again, still unsure.

"Come on," she purred, running a hand over his cheek. "I don't have cooties anymore, James."

I bit the inside of my cheek to keep myself from

crying out as he turned to face her. He swallowed hard, then inhaled deeply.

I watched with a weight in my chest, unable to breathe, unable to think.

He wasn't really going to do it, was he?

It's just a stupid dare. Why had I said that? He knew how Amber was. How difficult our relationship was.

Even still, he put a hand on her cheek, his eyes landing on her lips, and moved his head forward in what felt like slow motion. Their foreheads connected and he brushed his mouth against hers softly. She closed her eyes, tilting her chin toward his, deepening their kiss.

The air dissipated from my lungs, and I was suddenly light-headed.

I stood and their kiss ended abruptly.

James pulled away from Amber, his eyes finding me.

"You okay?" Eric studied me.

If I answered, or dared to open my mouth, I was sure I was going to scream. Instead, I moved forward, across the deck, and into the house.

I rushed up the stairs, tears stinging my eyes, and into the bathroom. I slammed the door shut with all my might, needing to take my anger out on something inanimate, and flipped on the faucet.

I stared at myself in the mirror—red faced, tear-filled eyes, frizzy blonde curls splayed in every direction. Why was I this way? Why could I never just let loose like Amber? Why couldn't I admit the truth, even to myself?

What was the truth anyway?

I splashed water over my face, contemplating staying

in the bathroom for the rest of the night if it meant I didn't have to face any of them ever again.

Maybe I'd stay in there until they were all in bed, and then I'd just leave. Make no opportunity for someone to stop me.

Would they stop me?

Maybe I was just the one dragging this weekend down. Everyone seemed lighter now that Amber was—

The door eased open and I switched the water off, squaring my shoulders as I prepared myself for what was to come.

A swish of light-brown hair told me who it was before I saw his face. His hand gripped the door, his expression troubled and stormy.

He shut the door behind him, closing us in the bathroom.

"You okay?"

How dare he ask me that.

"Why would you do that, Miles?" I kept my voice steady. In control.

He looked off to the side, his eyes unfocused, and when he spoke, he squeezed them shut. "I know you won't believe me, but I was doing that for you."

I opened my mouth and then shut it again, having prepared myself for a completely different answer. "Wh-what?"

"I needed you to know. Needed you to see for yourself."

"See what?" I curled my upper lip in disgust. Was this all some kind of game to him?

"How you feel about him."

"James?"

He gave a half nod.

"Not this again." I slapped my palms over my face. "I can't do this right now.

"Now you know. Whatever you're feeling right now —jealousy, anger, rage—sit with it. Feel it. That's as real as it gets."

"Why do you care so much, Miles? Why are you doing this?"

He pursed his lips, tucking a piece of hair behind his ear. "You just answered your own question. *Because* I care. I care about you. I want you to be happy. I want you to finally start making decisions for yourself. Life's too short for you to hide out anymore. So, be mad at me all you want, but the way I see it, I just did you a massive favor."

"A favor? Because you just had my best friend kiss my little sister? Yeah, thanks a ton."

"Yes. Because now you can deal with your feelings rather than hiding from them, Colbie. Whatever they are for James—"

"James doesn't like me. I wish everyone would stop saying that."

"Forget about his feelings for a minute. How do *you* feel about him?"

I thought long and hard, replaying the kiss in my head until I was practically dizzy. It made me furious to see them together. And confused.

But it wasn't because I was jealous.

153

That truth sat firmly in my gut.

It was because what had just unfolded was a shattering reminder that I had no one to kiss me that way. That maybe I never would again.

I trailed my gaze up to meet Miles's eyes slowly, swallowing hard, the truth balancing on my tongue. "James is my best friend. Nothing more. I've never seen him that way."

His chest puffed with a deep inhale.

"So, now you know."

"Now I know."

His smile was small. The sound of footsteps on the stairs interrupted us and, before I had a chance to think about my next move, someone was knocking on the door.

"What?" I called.

"It's me. Is everything okay?"

I tensed at the sound of his voice. "I'm fine, James. I just need to go to sleep."

"A-are you sure? Can I come in? We should talk."

I moved past Miles and swung the door open. He stood in front of me, the skin around his eyes crinkling with worry.

"There's nothing to talk about. See? I'm fine. I swear. Just tired."

"So, you didn't storm off because of what just happened?"

"No." I rubbed my eyes. "I just didn't want to play anymore. It was a stupid game anyway."

"We were having fun, Colb." Amber was climbing up

the stairs, her voice whiny, words slightly slurred. "Where'd you go? Come back and play with us."

"I'm done. You guys play."

It was then James spied Miles, who'd been hidden from view behind the wall next to the sink. "You're going to bed too?" Something darkened in his expression.

"Yeah, probably." Miles yawned. "Beauty rest and all."

"You guys are no fun!" Amber pouted, puffing out her bottom lip as she slipped an arm around James's waist. The sight of it caused something in me to snap.

"Or maybe we just don't feel like acting like teenagers and embarrassing ourselves is the best way to have fun."

The room fell silent, everyone waiting for Amber to respond. She was still for a while, her eyes locked on mine. Finally, she opened her mouth, her words cutting like knives. "What the hell would you know about fun, anyway? What have you *ever* known about fun? God, you're such a downer all the time."

James didn't defend me, though he looked conflicted, his gaze flicking back and forth between the two of us.

"Well, maybe, *just maybe* this weekend wasn't meant to be all about fun, Amber. Did you ever think of that? This weekend was for me. And for Phil. But you never think about anyone but yourself, do you?"

Her forehead wrinkled. "Oh, stop kidding yourself. This weekend was for you to throw a final pity party before people stop believing you're actually grieving."

I sucked in a sharp breath, the pain as real as if I'd been punched.

"Okay, stop. Colbie, please talk to me. Let's go and get some space. Clear our heads." James put an arm up in front of Amber, extending a hand for me, but that didn't stop my sister from laying out everything she wanted to say.

"You're so obsessed with Phil, even now, because it keeps people doting on you, Colbie. I see straight through it. Why the hell would you come here with these three guys, who are too nice to tell you no, to celebrate an anniversary that doesn't exist? With a guy who is long since gone? You weren't even together that long. You couldn't just stay home? You had to make it this big production—"

"*Enough.*" Miles's voice was commanding, but I was already moving. I shoved past her, smacking my shoulder into hers, and turned toward Eric's room.

"Don't be here when I wake up in the morning, Amber. And find somewhere else to stay. You can't stay with me."

"Gladly." She huffed.

With that, I slammed the door shut, leaving the three of them out in the hall, and threw myself onto my bed, curling up into a ball and letting the tears fall.

Tears of anger, bitterness, and confusion.

Tears for Phil.

For me.

For all that I'd lost.

When I'd nearly dozed off, the door opened and I looked over my shoulder, sniffling. "Go away."

"It's my room." Eric's voice was soft. He didn't acknowledge my tears, didn't force me to talk about what had happened or how I was feeling. Instead, he moved toward the bed. In his eyes, there was a question.

When I needed him most, without me having to say anything, he knew just what to do. It was what we'd done for each other so often over the past year.

I rolled over, no longer looking at him as I felt him lift the covers. He slipped into my bed, his body curling around me, one arm sliding around my waist. He held me tight, almost too tight, as I shook with silent sobs.

He didn't say a word, just let me cry, and held me until we both fell asleep.

CHAPTER EIGHTEEN

The next morning, as I'd asked, Amber was gone before I awoke. I didn't ask where she'd slept, where she'd gone, or where she was going.

The men stayed behind, helping me clean up the house before checking out. Everyone was quiet, uncomfortably so, as no one seemed to have any idea what to say about the night before or how to bring it up.

I offered a million apologies inside my head to James, to Miles too, about the way I'd acted—the fighting, the storming off, the anger when I'd basically given James permission to do what had hurt me the most—but I couldn't bear to speak them out loud.

If we managed never to speak about any of it again, maybe it would be like it hadn't happened.

At half past noon, we unloaded our bags back in my driveway. I wanted things to be different. They *should've* been different. I should've been thanking them for coming. Thanking them for being there for me, but I couldn't find the words.

They looked as if they wanted to say more too—Miles and James especially—but they didn't.

Couldn't, maybe.

So, instead, I hugged them all in the driveway, hoping my body was saying at least part of what I wanted to say, when I couldn't yet form the words.

Eric was the last to say goodbye, with a long hug and a look of understanding, but before he could leave, I stopped him, thankful he was the one person things weren't awkward with at the moment.

"Do you have plans today?"

"Work, sleep, repeat." He grinned. "Why? Did you have something else in mind?"

I raised a brow. "Actually, I was hoping we could go see the Tanners."

"Today?"

"Before I chicken out or it drives me mad."

His gaze shot toward the sky, obviously thinking, and eventually fell back down to meet mine. "Okay."

"Are you sure? Do we need to wait until you get off work?"

"If this is important to you, I will make it work. Should we call them first?"

"I'm worried they'll make up an excuse for us not to come if we do. Or just flat out ignore us. If we tip them off, they could make it harder for us to ever catch them at home. I think surprising them is the best plan we have."

He thought it over, and for a moment, I worried he'd

say no, but eventually he nodded, patting the hood of his car. "Okay. Get in."

"I should clean up first." I checked my phone. "Do you mind waiting?"

"Not at all. That gives me time to get some work in. I need to make a few of my more urgent phone calls anyway."

AN HOUR LATER, I'd showered and freshened up, applied minimal makeup to my face and styling cream to my unruly hair. I put on a sundress and sandals, trying not to worry about my appearance too much, though I couldn't help the fantasy playing out in my mind where they'd suddenly have a change of heart and welcome me into their home—into their lives—with open arms. Would a nice dress make that happen? Doubtful, but maybe not impossible.

I walked out of my bedroom, slinging my purse—the letter tucked safely inside—over my shoulder.

In the living room, Eric was on the couch, laptop resting on his thighs as he balanced the phone between his shoulder and ear.

"Come on, Bryan, that's ridiculous. Maybe for a prime location, but look at where it's at. And that bathroom? No way you're getting over what we're offering you. It needs to be gutted." He laughed dryly. "Okay. Yep, you talk to them. I just can't promise my clients aren't going to walk away in the meantime. They've already got their eye on another one on Cedar Point."

He paused again, typing something into his computer. "Six more hours, that's all I'm saying, and I don't think they're going to counter. They're all in here. Final offer." Another pause as he saw me walk in, his eyes lighting up as he closed his laptop. "Yep. Okay. Call me back." He ended the call and slipped his phone into his pocket, whistling. "Damn, Blondie. You clean up nice."

I rolled my eyes at him playfully. "You ready to go?"

"As ever." He shoved his laptop into his bag, tucking his phone into his pocket, and followed me out the door.

Once we were on our way, he tossed me his phone. "Want to pick the music?"

"Oh, you're actually going to let me this time? Twice in a row?"

He chuckled. "I'm feeling generous."

I scrolled through the music downloaded on his phone, before deciding on an Adele album.

"Did you hit shuffle or play?"

"Shuffle."

His lip twitched, and I sighed.

"What? Say it."

"It's just... If you hit play, they go in order."

I gave him a quirky, knowing grin. "Would you like them to go in order?"

"I guess it doesn't matter."

I giggled, picking up the phone and pressing play. "There you go."

He cut a glance at me. "See, isn't that better? The way the artist intended it."

"Oh, yes. So much better."

His smile was warm and contagious, sending waves of calm throughout my core.

"So, last night was...weird."

"Understatement of the century." I pressed the back of my head into the headrest, scooting forward in my seat.

"You and Amber really don't get along, do you?"

"It's complicated, I guess. We were close growing up, but then, after our mom died, she kind of went wild. And I..."

"Didn't," he finished.

"Right. Jerry had his hands full trying to raise us, while dealing with his own loss, and I just felt bad for him, honestly. We were never really close, but he was the only thing we had left that felt like a parent. I was sixteen and Amber was only fourteen, and I knew that..." I bit my lip.

"That what?"

"That..." I hated to even say the words, knowing how pathetic they'd sound. "That he had no real reason to stay if he didn't want to. And if he left us, I wasn't sure what would happen. Where we would go."

"You thought he was going to walk away from you?" The heartbreak of the statement was evident in his tone.

"I worried about it, yeah. So, I tried to do my best to never give him a reason to. I cleaned up Amber's messes, helped her hide stuff from him, took care of things."

"You were just a kid, too."

"You stop being a kid the moment you lose a parent." I stole a glance out the window, watching the trees zip past.

"Still. That wasn't fair to you." He reached across the center console and rested his hand on my thigh for a brief second. "When Phil told me how you'd lost both your parents, I couldn't even imagine. But you don't show it. I think if I'd gone through what you have, I'm not even sure I'd still be standing."

"Some days, I don't feel like I am." My vision blurred with tears, and I refused to turn my head to look at him. "But it's what my parents would've wanted. What Phil would've wanted. I can't just give up."

He was quiet for a moment, perhaps giving me time to compose myself. As a song ended and the car filled with silence, he asked, "So, that's why you don't get along? Because you've always had to take care of her when she was rebelling."

"We're just very different people. I love my sister, don't get me wrong, but it's hard to be around her. She's always exactly like she was last night. Wild, carefree, spontaneous. And damn the consequences. That's not me. It was exhausting trying to keep her together during school, and then, even when I got out, I was always having to drive home and fix a mess because I worried about what would happen if Jerry left her. I would've had to take her in, to raise her, and I was barely getting by on my own."

"So you resent her for taking away those final years of

your childhood? For not giving you space and time to grieve when you needed it."

I'd never heard it put into those words before, but yeah, I guessed that was it. "It sounds so selfish."

"Stop it. Look, you were both just kids doing your best, but she's not a kid anymore, Blondie. And it looks like you're still having to clean up her messes. It's you she ran to when she needed something yet again."

I nodded slowly, then tried to force a joke. "Bet you're glad you're an only child."

His smile was small, and I realized my mistake as soon as I said it. Phil was the closest thing Eric ever had to a brother. And now he was gone.

"He loved you, you know?" I whispered, the words making my chest constrict. Why was it that all roads led back to Phil?

"I know." His voice cracked, though I made no mention of it. "But that doesn't mean we didn't drive each other crazy sometimes. I get it."

"I shouldn't complain. She's all I have left. Well, besides Jerry."

His hand slipped over toward me again, his palm opening, fingers locking with mine. "They're not all you have, Colbie. You have me. And Miles." He rolled his eyes at the mention of his name. "And James. Though he might be your brother-in-law before too long." He released my hand and elbowed me, but I didn't laugh.

"Gross. Don't even joke about that."

His smile faded. "Seriously, though. You aren't alone. You know that, right?"

IF YOU'RE READING THIS…

"I do." I wasn't sure if it was a lie. In all reality, of course I wasn't alone, but no one in my life knew what my loss felt like. Not even Eric. My entire future had been ripped away in a split second. He still had a future. Phil was a *part* of his life, albeit a huge one. He was my *entire* life.

"So, elephant in the room, what are you planning to say to his parents?"

"I don't know," I admitted. "I'm going to let them read the letter, I think. Though…it scares me to think I won't get it back."

"So, read it to them. Or show them a picture of it."

"That's not a bad idea." I was grateful he didn't tell me I was ridiculous to think they'd try to keep it. In truth, we had no idea what my in-laws were capable of.

Almost-in-laws.

I pulled out my phone and the letter, unfolding it and snapping a picture. This way, the letter remained between Phil and me. No one else ever had to touch it if I didn't want them to.

"And then I'm going to ask if they know what he might've meant by any of that."

Eric nodded. "I hope you get the answers you're looking for."

"I hope we both do."

Two hours later, we pulled down the Tanners' long driveway. It was a big Southern house with apple trees in the yard and oversized columns on the front porch. The house was bright white, perfectly manicured, and behind it, they had stables and a garden complete with a fountain. The first time Phil ever brought me here, I couldn't believe it. The house and its land were straight out of a magazine.

I'd known he came from money, but even still, there's knowing and there's *knowing*.

This time wasn't much better.

I stared around in awe, a knot of worry in my gut as Eric pulled the car to a stop and looked over at me. "You're sure about this?"

"As sure as I can be." I hoped he didn't see the fear in my eyes. I wanted to be braver than this.

I pushed my door open before I could allow myself to second-guess, and he locked his hand with mine as we made our way up the walk and toward the large front door. There was nothing romantic about the gesture, simply a show of support. He was there for me, as I was for him.

Whatever we were about to find out, it could change so much.

I rang the doorbell and he released my hand, lifting it to my back. We exchanged another worried glance just before the door swung open.

Phil's mom stood in front of me, her blonde hair perfectly curled, makeup flawlessly painted on. She eyed me as if she didn't recognize me at first, then her gaze fell to Eric and her jaw dropped.

"Hi, Mrs. Tanner." I hoped I sounded more confident than I felt.

She cut a glance to me. "What are you doing here?"

"I was hoping I could talk to you for a few minutes."

"We have nothing left to discuss, Colbie." She moved to shut the door, but Eric spoke up.

"Please. Please just hear her out. We won't be here long."

"And why would I do that?" She stared down at him.

"Because he would've wanted you to."

Phil would've wanted her to do so much more than she had, but I didn't argue. Instead, I watched Calliope as she studied Eric, a boy she'd raised practically as her own son. A boy who'd spent summers and evenings playing on the lawn with her own child.

How could she turn him away?

She sighed, looking like she'd rather do anything else, and stepped back. "I have a video call in twenty minutes, so let's make this fast."

"Thank you." I scurried past her, Eric's hand still on my back as we walked into the house. It was light, bright, and airy—a chilling contrast to the darkness I saw behind its owner's eyes.

She didn't offer us anything to drink or even to take a seat. Instead, she folded her arms there in the foyer and said, "So, what's this about?" She was only looking at Eric, as if I didn't exist.

"At our wedding, Phil and I had a box where people could leave letters for us to open on our one-year anniversary." *I wouldn't have to explain this to you if you'd both-*

167

ered to show up. "This weekend, I opened them and..." I pulled out my phone with shaking hands. "There was a letter from Phil."

Calliope looked at me for the first time, her complexion blanching. "What?"

"I wanted to read it to you."

She swallowed hard, her eyes bouncing around the room, trying and failing to hide how badly she wanted to hear what I had to say.

"Go on."

I opened the photo and began reading the letter aloud to her.

"'If you're reading this, it means I'm already gone.'" I looked up to see her leaning in farther, trying to read my screen. "'I'm so sorry about that. It was selfish of me to love you, Colbie. Selfish of me to marry you when I knew what I'd be doing to you. When I knew I couldn't protect you. It would be selfish of me now to ask you to forgive me, when I don't deserve an ounce of your forgiveness. But that's what I want to do.'"

I paused, trying to collect myself before going on. When I spoke again, my voice was shakier, my breaths ragged.

"'I hope I'm still with you by the time you open this letter. I hope that you know the truth about me—who I am and what I've done. And I hope that, by some miracle, I'm still right by your side. But if I'm not—if I'm gone—if I never see you again, know how much I loved you. Know how badly I wanted to protect you from all of this. And know that, with my last breath, I'll be thinking of you. Love always, Phil.'"

When I looked up, my vision was blurred with tears, her facial features like a kaleidoscope in front of me.

Her lips were pressed into a thin line, arms folded across her chest, one finger tapping her bicep. "That's all?"

"I... What?"

"It was a letter to you. Nothing in there at all to me. Or his father. His family. His blood. I don't understand why you would bring that here, other than to rub it in our faces."

"I'm sorry if that's how it feels, but I promise you that's not why I'm here. I wanted to ask you if you might know why he thought he was in danger. What exactly was he trying to protect me from?"

"How on earth would I know that?" she snapped.

"I thought you might. He said *if you're reading this, I'm already gone.* It makes it sound like he knew he was going to die, doesn't it? Like he knew something bad was going to happen?"

"Where is the *actual* letter?" She folded her arms again, moving away from me to pace the room. "How do I know it even exists?"

"I... I don't have it. Just the picture."

"Well, don't you think that might be something his parents want to hold on to? His *actual* family?"

My stomach flipped. "I *am* his actual family, Mrs. Tanner. And, like you said, the letter is addressed to me.

Not you. I know you didn't approve of our relationship—"

She scoffed. "If that's what you want to call it."

Not wanting to add fuel to the fire, I lowered my voice. "I loved your son very, very much. I miss him every day. I know you're hurting and, if you don't want to help me—"

"Help you?" She threw her head back with a laugh. "Well, you just about *helped* yourself, didn't you? You were just seconds away from helping yourself to quite a little fortune, hmm?"

The words stung, and I swallowed down my pride. "I never cared about your money. I was happy to sign a prenup. It was never about that for me, and Phil knew that."

"Phil *believed* that, anyway."

"What in God's name is going on here?" Nelson Tanner rounded the corner, his perfectly styled salt-and-pepper hair and dark, fitted suit demanding all the attention he believed he was entitled to. He wore rings on every finger, a pinched grimace on his face.

"Colbie here apparently got a letter from Phil. She thinks he was in some sort of trouble." Calliope said it as if it was the most ludicrous thing in the world.

"What? What kind of letter? Where is it?" His gaze fell from me to Eric and back again. "Hello, Eric."

"Mr. Tanner." Eric shuffled half a step closer to me, his warmth helping me to find my footing in the conversation.

"He left it for me to find on our one-year anniversary.

In it, he said he hoped he could protect me from *all of this*. And that if I was reading it *he was already gone*."

His eyes widened, but when he spoke, the words that came out were far from what I expected. "What exactly are you trying to imply about my son?"

"I—what? Nothing. I'm just worried that he was in danger. I wanted you to both know about it, to see if there might be something you could tell me that—"

"Now you listen here." He wagged a finger in my direction, his face flushing red. "Whatever you've got in your head, I suggest you forget about it. Don't you dare go running around trying to spread rumors about my boy without him here to defend himself."

"I'm not spreading anything. I'm worried about him. I want to know if someone hurt him."

His nostrils flared. "His death was an accident. If there was anything to tell, we'd know about it and it would be none of your concern."

"What about the broken champagne bottle on the floor that day? What if someone had attacked him? Or what if—"

"My son was high the day he died. His blood alcohol level was elevated. I'm—"

"*What?*"

He pursed his lips, as if he didn't have time to explain any of this, but it was all news to me.

"I'm sure any of those things would explain a broken champagne bottle better than a supposed attack. The police all agree, which you would know if it was any of your business. No one tried to hurt him. He just needed to get drunk and high on God knows what in order to go through with your marriage."

"That doesn't make any sense. He—"

"Now, what right do you have to come here and upset his mother and me? I told you that night at the hospital that we never wanted to see you again, and I told you the same thing at the funeral, which you're lucky we let you come to at all. I meant what I said. You don't want to make us your enemies."

Eric gripped my arm. "We'll just go."

"You knew better than to bring her here," Nelson sputtered, looking at Eric as if it was the ultimate betrayal.

"She has a right to ask questions."

They were toe to toe then, and it broke my heart to see. *Phil wouldn't have wanted this.* I pulled him back, turning toward the door, my chest aching.

"Oh, actually—" Calliope spoke up just before I reached the door, Eric a step behind. I spun around, hating the hope I felt in my chest. "Before you go, I have something for you."

"Something?"

"Yes. Just a minute."

Nelson followed her from the room, huffing as she went.

Eric turned to me. His eyes said it all—this had been a bad idea, he'd tried to warn me, I should've listened—but he was too much of a gentleman to ever say the words aloud.

I turned away from him, no longer able to meet his

eyes, and walked toward the built-in bookcase on the wall. It was adorned with pictures and mementos from over the years—business mergers, family vacations, Theo's wedding, Phil, Theo, and Nelson on the golf course.

"We can bolt if you want to. You don't have to put yourself through any more of this." Eric was closer than I'd anticipated, his voice low.

I thought about it as my eyes scanned the photos, nearly agreeing when I froze. I leaned forward, trying to get a better look at the woman in the picture, wrapped in Phil's embrace.

What the...

"Eric, look..." I pointed to the photo, drawing his attention to it.

"Here it is." Calliope reappeared in the hallway, her heels clicking against the marble floors as she made her way to me, holding out a large manila envelope.

I could hardly think.

Hardly breathe.

"What is this?" Eric asked, when I hadn't come up with the brainpower to do so myself. My mind was still on the picture.

"It's an eviction notice."

Her words brought me back to reality as her eyes twinkled with delight.

"A...*what?*"

"Sixty days. Should be more than enough."

"You're..." I twirled the envelope in my hands. "You're kicking me out of my home?"

"*Our* home." She grinned hungrily, the victory clear in her eyes. "It was given to Phil conditionally per the terms of his upcoming partnership agreement. You have no rights to it."

"Y-you can't do this. This isn't what he would've wanted. It's my home. It's all that I have—"

She held up a hand, cutting me off. "I don't think you're in any position to tell me what *my* son would've wanted. In any case, we've been unnecessarily generous by letting you stay there as long as you have. You've had a full year in a home you had no rights to."

"It was his home. Our home." Tears cascaded down my cheeks, but I no longer cared. It was as if I'd stepped into an alternate universe. Our home was all I had left of him. All I had left of us.

"No. I'm afraid it wasn't. He didn't marry you, so the contract is now null and void, making the property ours. Not yours. We've had those papers drawn up for months, but hadn't gotten around to getting them delivered to you. But since you showed up on our doorstep, there's no time like the present." She clasped her hands together in front of her. "Now, if you'll be on your way. As I said, I do have a call to be on."

"What do you mean? What does that mean *he didn't marry me so the contract is void*? I don't understand. What contract?"

"Oh, as if you didn't know." She wrinkled her nose.

"The partnership agreement." Nelson clearly had other things to attend to, already on his phone and speaking to me as if he was ordering lunch, rather than delivering such a devastating blow. "My son didn't stand to inherit his share of the company until he married." His eyes flicked to me. "Which he never did."

The room spun, the air suddenly sucked from my lungs.

I was too hot and too cold.

Too dizzy.

Too still.

A pair of hands were on me, and suddenly, the world was too bright.

Next thing I knew, Eric was buckling me into his car and I had no idea how we'd made it there.

CHAPTER NINETEEN

E ric gripped the steering wheel so tightly it looked as if he might tear the leather. I couldn't bring myself to say anything, for fear that if I spoke, my worst fears would come spilling out.

I had nowhere to go.

I'd just gotten in a huge fight with my sister and my best friend.

I should've never moved out of my apartment. I waited until the last possible minute, because I was terrified something would go wrong, but eventually Phil convinced me.

You're my home, he'd said. *You should be here.*

Our last three months together had been spent within those walls, making memories that were supposed to last me a lifetime.

Now, what?

There was nothing I could do.

I had sixty days to say goodbye once again, and I

wasn't sure I'd make it through.

"You know you can come stay with me." Eric broke the silence. "Or…if you don't want to, I'll help you find a place. There are a couple two bedrooms I have listed right now that—"

"I can't afford to buy a house, Eric. There's no way I'll qualify on my own."

"Then, move in with me."

"I can't do that."

"Why not?"

"I'm not going to impose on your life any more than I already have—"

"You haven't—"

"I have. Don't think I haven't noticed the fact that you've stopped dating almost entirely because you've been spending your weekends and evenings with me for the better part of a year. All of you. It isn't fair to you. I'm not your problem. You all deserve to have lives and futures and families and—"

"Don't do that." He shot a stern look my way. "Don't act like you're a burden. I'm here out of choice."

"Because Phil would've wanted you to, I know. And you've been such a good friend to me, but I can't keep taking up your life—"

"*You're not taking up my life!*" He stressed the words. "Blondie, if I wanted to be dating, I would. Did you ever think maybe I just like spending time with you? That maybe this is exactly where I want to be?"

I stared at him, shocked by the confession.

"I like spending time with you. Not just because Phil

would've wanted it, but because *I* want it. I want to spend time with you. Maybe that's not how it started, but that's how it is now. As much as I've helped you this year, you've helped me just the same. You were there for me when my entire life fell apart. You helped me get through my courses and get my license. Hell, you helped me design my business cards."

He laughed under his breath, recalling the many arguments we had over the right placement, I was sure. "Without you, I'd still be getting drunk every night, sleeping in until the afternoon, and trying to keep a dead-end job. I don't want that life anymore. I thought I'd made that clear, but obviously not, so let me do it now. That is not what I want. *This* is what I want. Right here. I'm here. And I'm not going to let you go through this or anything else alone." He slid his hand across to me again, resting it on my leg. "Like it or not."

My head swirled with emotion from all that he was saying. Was it true? Could he really be less than burdened by me after all I'd needed from him this year?

I moved my hand over his, resting it on top. "Thank you. I'm really glad to have you here. And...I feel the same way." It was all I could think to say, though it felt wrong and weak and feeble compared to all he'd said.

"Good." A small smile played on his lips. "Then we're going to start packing your things. You can move in with me while you find a place. No arguments. I have the extra bedroom, and you'll be safe there. No need for creepy roommates or shady apartments."

I shook my head. "Fine. No arguments. Thank you,

Eric. Seriously. It means a lot to me. And I promise, it'll just be for a few months. Three tops."

"It can be for as long as you need."

We left it at that.

"They're awful people. They've always been, but…" He was staring straight ahead, his jaw tight as he said it. "If he could see them now…"

"Did you know?" I turned toward him, suddenly reminded of the other news I'd received, and he shot a glance at me. "Did you know about the fact that we had to get married for him to get part of the company?"

He swallowed, shaking his head. "I'm learning there's a lot I didn't know about him."

"Why wouldn't he have told us?"

"Maybe it didn't matter to him…" He offered, but it was halfhearted. "Maybe he didn't want you to think exactly what you're thinking now."

"You know what I'm thinking?" I wasn't being stubborn. I genuinely wanted to know if what I was thinking wasn't crazy.

"He wasn't only marrying you to get the company. He wouldn't have."

Spot on.

He could read me so well.

"You can't know that. You just said you're finding out so much about him now and—"

"But I do know this: he could've married anyone. He dated other people before you. If he just wanted to marry someone, he had plenty of opportunities. I don't buy that for a second, and you shouldn't either. He cared about you. Loved you."

I nodded, because I truly needed to hear it, but it wasn't sinking in. "I just wish he would've been honest. Why would they want him to be married anyway? They hated me so much, why wouldn't they just change that rule if they thought I was marrying him for his money?"

"It wouldn't have mattered. Phil had his mind made up. That would only have made a difference if he were marrying you for the company."

I nodded just as another thought occurred to me. "What about the drugs? Did you know about that? Did you see him take anything that day?"

He didn't answer right away. "He wasn't a saint by any means. I know he was drinking that day. Pretty heavily, too. But I didn't know he took anything other than that, no. For all we know, they were just saying that to make you feel more out of the loop. I wouldn't put it past them."

"I just don't understand why he would—" Another more urgent thought occurred to me then. There were so many shocks at the Tanners' it was hard to keep them straight.

"What? What is it?"

"That girl." My eyes were wide as I stared at him, watching for some sign of recognition. "In the picture. Do you know her?"

His brows drew down. "You mean Paige?"

"I guess so. The blonde in the picture with Phil."

"Paige." He confirmed. "His ex. What about her?"

My body chilled. "H-his ex? They dated?" When he nodded, I asked, "When?"

"A few years ago, I guess. She was the last one I remember before you. The last serious one, anyway. Why? Do you know her?"

"Um, no, not exactly, but someone else does."

He turned his head slightly, listening.

"I saw a picture of Paige recently, only it wasn't because of Phil. She's... Eric, she's Miles's sister."

His eyes widened. "What?"

"You didn't know?"

"I had no idea."

"Did Phil?"

"Did he know she was Miles's sister?" He seemed skeptical. "I doubt it. He didn't know Miles, did he?"

"I don't know. But what are the odds?"

"What do you mean?"

"Well, I told you Miles acted strangely when he met Phil the day of the wedding. What if they already knew each other?"

He was quiet. "Maybe. It would be a weird coincidence."

"What happened to her?"

He shrugged casually. "I think they just grew apart. Phil never really said. She was around for a while and then she wasn't. Shortly after, you came along."

"No, I, um... I meant how did she die?"

He twisted to look at me, his brows crashing together. "Wait, what? Paige is dead?"

"That's what Miles told me."

He blanched, smoothing a palm over his face. "Shit. I had no idea."

I pulled out my phone and searched her name, now that I had a first to go with the last.

Paige West death Nashville, TN

The first article was a hit, a news article from three years ago.

"Here we go..."

"What'd you find?"

I read through it quickly, the blood draining from my face as I shook my head. "It's awful. She was found in the woods. Blunt force trauma..." I covered my mouth with a shaking hand. "They never found out who did it."

He squeezed his eyes shut. "*Shit.*"

"I feel so bad I didn't know. Poor Miles..."

"No wonder he doesn't like to talk about his past."

I zoned out, reading through the article again and, before I knew it, we were pulling into my driveway. When the car came to a stop, I put my phone down on my lap. "Thank you again for going with me."

"I'll always help you."

"I know." My cheeks flamed. "I couldn't have done it alone."

His smile was warm but small. I could see that he wanted to say more, but he didn't. Wouldn't. "I can come by after work and help you start to pack, if you want. Or whatever you need."

"You aren't sick of me yet?" I laughed.

"Stop doing that."

"I'm sorry. That would be really nice, actually."

"Then I'll be here."

He stared at me, his eyes dancing with whatever he was contemplating saying, but eventually, they fell to his lap. I turned away, reaching for the door handle.

As he pulled away moments later, I fought against the sobs clawing at my chest, my lungs. I wanted to break down. To give in and drown myself in alcohol and bad television, but I had to stay busy.

Phil was counting on me.

Eric was counting on me.

I was counting on myself.

The truth had to come out.

CHAPTER TWENTY

I was in the kitchen, my laptop open in front of me on the table and a half-empty bag of trail mix next to it, when Eric returned that evening.

"Blondie?"

Something was wrong.

I knew it from the tone of his voice, even before I saw him.

"Yeah?" I shoved myself up from the table just as he appeared. He placed two bags of fast food on the table, looking me over.

"Are you okay?"

"Why wouldn't I be?"

He hesitated, a worried look in his eyes.

"Eric, what is it?"

"Have you been outside?"

A rock sank in my gut.

"You've got a flat tire." His eyes searched mine. "I was

worried that..." He swiped a palm over his face. "I was worried."

I darted past him, despite him yelling after me, and rushed out the door and to the driveway. Sure enough, before I'd even reached the car, I could see the tire sitting flat on the rim.

I bent over, trying to get a better look at it as anger and confusion swelled in my chest. "What the hell? It was fine earlier." How was I going to get to work? How long would this take to fix?

He placed a hand on my shoulder. "Maybe you drove over a nail or something. It happens."

"I haven't gone anywhere." I ran a hand through my hair, trying to think. "Am I supposed to call my insurance company? Or a tow truck? Phil would've been the one to handle this before..." I tried to slow my erratic breathing.

"No, it's okay. No big deal. Do you have a spare?"

"Um, I don't think so."

He moved around the car, popping the trunk from the driver's side. I couldn't see what he was doing, still staring at the tire in a complete state of overwhelm.

He slammed the trunk shut, hands on his hips. "You just have a donut. You don't have to work until Wednesday, right? In the morning, I can run you down to get a spare and I'll help you put it on. It's too dark tonight."

"Thanks," I mumbled, not really listening. I ran my fingers over the tire slowly. "Hey, you don't think someone...did this on purpose, do you?"

His brows drew down. "Someone? Like who?"

I stared around my street, spying a dark SUV I didn't recognize. Had the neighbors gotten a new car, or was it...

"Forget it." I waved it off. It was late and hot, and I was exhausted. This was ridiculous. "Let's go back inside."

In the kitchen a few minutes later, he tapped my messy bun as he walked past me to grab the ketchup out of the fridge. "It's going to be okay, Blondie. Just a flat. Happens to the best of us."

I puffed out a breath, resting my cheek in my palm as I fought to change the subject. "I know. How was work?"

"Two offers accepted, and another one put in. Now we wait."

I grinned up at him as he came to sit down next to me. "That's incredible. Congratulations."

He looked down, pretending to be humble all of a sudden, and turned his attention to the bag to pull out our burgers and fries.

"Did you remember—"

"No onions," he confirmed, placing the food in front of me. "You know I got you, Blondie." He wagged the bottle of ketchup. "And extra ketchup for your fries."

I popped a fry into my mouth. "You're the best."

He took a sip of his soda. "So, whatcha working on?"

"I'm looking into Paige a little bit, trying to learn more about her."

"And what have you learned?"

"A lot, actually. Her family is rich. Like stupid rich. They own some hotel chain."

"No kidding?" His eyes narrowed at me. "You'd never know it, talking to Miles."

"Yeah, but he doesn't talk about them much, does he?"

"It explains how he's able to do the band full time. I mean, it's not like they're touring or anything."

I ignored the comment, because I knew Eric thought Miles's job was unreasonable for someone in their midthirties.

"Yeah, I guess so. I get the feeling his family is a touchy subject. Maybe it's because of what happened to her."

"Makes sense." He unwrapped his burger. "Are you going to ask him about it?"

"I don't really know how to. But...I keep thinking. What if that's what Phil was talking about in his letter? Maybe whatever happened to Paige, maybe he thought the person might be after him. Maybe they were involved in something or...or they saw something."

"What? Like some...witness protection, Mafia stuff?"

"Do I sound as crazy as I feel?" I puffed out a breath, leaning forward into my hands over the table.

"Look, if it bothers you that much, maybe we should ask Miles."

I liked the way he'd said *we*. I wasn't alone in this. Just like the tire and so much else.

"I don't want to seem like we're confronting him. I just... Maybe he can clear things up." I pinched a piece of skin near my thumbnail.

"So, text him. See if he can come over, and we'll talk. I'm sure he'll be able to clear it up. No big deal."

"Yeah?"

"Yeah." He tossed a fry at me, laughing when my jaw dropped open.

"Jerk."

"You love me."

I shook my head, turning my attention to my phone and tapping out a message to Miles before I could chicken out.

His response came within minutes.

Be there in an hour.

IT WAS LESS than an hour before he arrived, in fact. We'd just cleaned up dinner and were sitting around the kitchen table when he walked into the room.

His eyes fell to Eric, then to me.

"Oh. Hey."

"Hey!" My smile was too bright. Too cheery after the awkwardness of the morning.

"What's...up? Everything okay?"

"Yeah, I just thought we could hang out."

He nodded, seeming to ease up a bit, and made his way to the table. "Hey, man."

Eric nodded at him. "You already eat? We just finished. I didn't know you were coming or I would've brought extra."

"I'm good." He waved him off. "James here too?"

I stiffened at the sound of his name. If he knew the three of us were together right now without him, it would hurt his feelings. But inviting him would just make this weirder right now.

Plus, I didn't want Miles to feel cornered.

"No. Not tonight. This is all sort of impromptu."

He hesitated, hearing something in my voice. "Yeah?"

I sank into the chair across from him and folded my hands in front of me, staring at my fingers. "I need to ask you something."

He swallowed, stealing a glance at Eric. "Sure."

"Was your sister named Paige? The one I saw the picture of."

After a breath, Miles said, "Yes..." His wary gaze danced between the two of us.

"And did your sister date Phil?"

Something shifted in his eyes. Darkened.

"I think you already know the answer to that question, or you wouldn't be asking."

I paused. "Why didn't you tell me?"

"I didn't think you'd want to know. How'd you find out anyway?"

"We went to his parents' house today. They had a picture of the two of them together."

"Sons of bitches." He scowled.

"I take it you aren't their biggest fan either."

He looked up at me from behind dark brows. "Our parents were friends growing up. They had some big falling out a few years ago, while Paige and Phil were dating. They haven't spoken to our family since she died. Didn't even come to the funeral."

It kept getting worse.

They just kept surprising me when I thought there was no room left to be surprised.

"I'm so sorry."

He swiped a hand through his hair, a finger getting caught in a tangle that he attempted to work out. "Was that your only question?"

"Not quite. I wondered... Did you come to our wedding knowing Phil would be there?"

"No." His answer was quick. His spine stiffened as he leaned into the table. "I had no idea it was his wedding until I got there."

"But you *did* know him? You knew who he was?"

"Try as I might to forget him."

"So that's why you acted strangely when he introduced himself to you."

"Yeah. Introduced himself, like he didn't know me. For your sake, probably. Didn't want any drama."

"Do you have any idea what happened to Paige?"

He pulled his hand free, his jaw tight, obviously caught off guard by the question. "I have some theories, yeah."

"Do you think that same person could've been after Phil? Do you think that's what he meant in the letter? Could they have been involved in something that put them both in danger?"

Eric leaned closer, waiting for his response, but Miles scoffed. "Doubtful."

"Why not?"

He shook his head. "Because the person I suspect did it, died that night."

My body ran cold, a headache beginning in my temple. "Phil?"

He met my eyes but didn't speak.

"You think he did something to Paige? You think he hurt her?"

He didn't nod, but he didn't need to. His eyes said it all. He ran his tongue over his bottom lip.

"Why?" I demanded. "Why would you think that?"

"He was the last person to see her. They were dating, and he didn't even bother to come to the funeral. The list goes on..."

"But you were friends. Or your families were. Didn't you just ask him?"

"I tried. I called. I came over. His parents protected him. They'd never let me see him. He wouldn't answer my calls. I had no idea where he was living when he wasn't at work. My parents tried too. They pushed the detectives working her case, paid for private investigators, but there was nothing to be found. It was as if all the evidence had been wiped clean." His final sentence was electric. Pointed. I understood exactly what he was saying.

"So, I finally saw my chance to approach him at the wedding, and I did, once you weren't around."

"What did he say?" Eric was hanging on his every word, sounding as weak as I felt.

"He said he'd tell me whatever I wanted to know, but

we had to get through the wedding." His eyes dropped to his hands on the table and then back up to me. "He told me how special you were, and how it would kill him if your day was ruined. He... He told me about your parents. How you'd already lost so much."

I clutched my stomach. The headache was throbbing now. I felt as if I might pass out.

"He swore if we made it through the wedding, the two of us could sit down and he'd answer whatever I wanted him to."

"And you believed him? After he'd been blowing you off for years?"

He shrugged one shoulder lazily. "I didn't have a choice. He was a lawyer. His parents own half the town. He told me it was my only chance to get answers, because if I messed up the wedding or dared to walk out, he'd pull every string he had to make sure he never had to answer any questions about her death, to make sure I never got the answers I was looking for."

"He basically blackmailed you..." An uncontrollable shudder swept through my body. "Why would you agree?"

"I didn't have a choice. I'd already met you. I wasn't going to ruin your wedding. I chose to trust him and... then...then none of it mattered anyway."

Tears blurred my eyes. "Miles, I'm so sorry. I had no idea... There has to be some explanation. The man I knew, the man I loved, he was never anything but kind. Loving. Gentle. He couldn't have hurt her."

"Why would you agree to play at his funeral after all

of that?" Eric asked.

"Because she asked me to." His answer was simple but powerful. He met my eyes again. "That was for you. It was never about him. No matter how I felt about him, you were innocent in it all."

I lowered my head. "This is all too much."

I thought then of what Eric had warned me, that if I went looking for answers, I might not like what I found.

I was starting to see that, just as I was starting to question if any of us knew Phil at all.

"At least you have your answers." Eric leaned closer to me across the table. "Now you know."

"Maybe that's what the letter meant. Maybe he was going to confess," Miles offered. "Maybe he was going to turn himself in."

"Maybe." My head was heavy. "I'm sorry, guys. I think I'm going to turn in for the night. I…need some time to process all of this."

"Are you sure?" Eric stood as I moved.

"I should go too." Miles pushed up from the table. "Let you get some sleep."

I didn't hear what Eric said back. I was too far away, across the house and behind my bedroom door within seconds. I collapsed on the bed, no longer feeling strong, but rather broken.

I had no idea who I'd nearly married.

No idea what secrets my friends were hiding from me.

And now, no idea what I was going to do with any of this.

CHAPTER TWENTY-ONE

*C*rash.

My eyes shot open, sunlight piercing through the curtains.

What was that? Had I imagined it?

I rolled over and grabbed my phone, checking to see if anyone had tried to call me to say they were coming over.

Nothing.

Shit.

I was trapped with no car. I stood from the bed, still wobbly on my feet as I tried to decide what to do without overreacting. I listened for the sounds of anyone moving through the house.

Nothing.

I puffed out a breath.

Probably just a dream.

I hadn't expected to fall asleep so easily the night before, but once I'd landed in my bed, the sadness and grief overtook me—much like the early days of loss. When all I'd ever wanted to do was sleep.

When I was in so much pain, I was sure it would never end.

When I was sure no one had ever hurt as much as I did, because how would they possibly still be able to function? How was anyone who had felt a loss like mine still walking around in society, rather than melded into their couch for the rest of eternity?

Even this morning, I felt the pain of it. An ever-present burning just north of my temples.

A pain that reminded me of all that had gone wrong.

I slipped out of the bedroom, stretching my hands over my head and making my way toward my bathroom.

Twisting the knob, my breathing hitched.

It was locked.

Why was it locked?

My body tensed, my chest caving in. I twisted it again.

"Just a sec."

Relief coursed through me first, then confusion.

"Eric?"

The door swung open and he stood in front of me, dressed in a button-down shirt and slacks for work, his hair still wet from a recent shower. I caught a hint of the fresh, woodsy cologne he wore so often. Floral notes and hints of cedar.

"Sorry. Just finishing up. I have a showing this morning. Will you be okay?"

"I... Um, yes. I...I didn't realize you were still here."

"I couldn't leave you last night. I knew how upset you were—after the tire and then...everything else. I thought you might wake up and want to talk or...you know, whatever."

"So you stayed?"

His eyes shifted, uncertainty peeking out from behind the clouds. "Is that okay?"

"Of course." A mischievous grin played on my lips. "We're about to be roomies, aren't we? Might as well get used to this."

A corner of his mouth upturned. "Might as well."

"Colbie?"

A voice came from behind me, and I spun around as Eric's gaze shot up to look over my shoulder.

"James?"

He stood at the end of the long hallway, dressed in blue scrubs.

"What are you doing here?"

"It's Tuesday." He said it as if it were the most obvious thing, and realization swept over me. The long weekend had my internal calendar all messed up. "Are we not going to the shelter?"

"Shoot. No. We are. I'm sorry. I overslept."

He couldn't stop his gaze from traveling between Eric and me and back again. We hadn't spoken since the morning before, and I didn't like where we'd left things. But this... This was good.

A little white flag, an olive branch, an extended hand.

It was my chance to finally move on, so I was going to take it.

"We'll have to take your car. Mine has a flat."

"I saw that. What happened?"

"No idea. We just noticed it last night."

"Need any help with it?"

"I'm going to help her with it." Eric looked at me. "I'll go pick up the tire while you're gone. I'll get it fixed today."

"Okay, thank you." I wanted to say more, but instead, I turned my attention back to a waiting James. "Let me just pull my hair up and brush my teeth, and then we'll go." I needed to shower, but it was no use. A day at the shelter meant I'd leave smelling worse than a usual day of work.

"Got it." His tone was clipped and he turned away.

So, maybe things weren't okay after all.

Eric touched my arm, his grip soft. "I'll see you later, okay?"

"Okay. Thanks for...everything."

He dipped his head slowly, his eyes warming, and then, he was gone.

***

LIKE I PROMISED JAMES, ten minutes later I was walking down the hall, my hair pulled back into a messy ponytail, and I was dressed in clean clothes, my teeth brushed and face washed.

I found him standing near the door, watching for me.

"You ready?"

"Yep. Let's go."

He pulled open the door and led the way to the car, keeping a pace several steps ahead of me. Once in the car and on the way, I scrolled through my phone, checking what I'd missed the night before.

Nothing important, that was for sure.

"So, Eric stayed over, hmm?" James tried to keep his voice casual, as if he couldn't care less, but I knew that wasn't the case. I could hear it, maybe for the first time.

"Yeah. We went to see Phil's parents yesterday, and he came back for dinner because I was upset. I went to bed early, but he stuck around to be sure I was okay."

"I take it the visit didn't go well, then?"

"You could say that." I paused, glancing out the window. "I'm, uh, being kicked out of our house and I found out that Phil needed to marry me in order to make partner."

"*What?*" The vein in his neck twitched.

"Yeah. I have sixty days to get out, and...yeah."

"I don't even know which question to ask first. How can they do that? Where will you go?"

I explained the situation quickly, glossing over the particularly painful parts. "So, I'm going to stay with Eric until I can find a place. I'll probably go back to renting an apartment for a while."

The air cooled quickly, his face turning to stone. "Oh."

"It's just temporary. He has an extra bedroom and, well, it's not like I have many options."

"You could always stay with me. You know that."

"I do know that. But your spare room is set up for

recording the podcast and I'd hate for you to have to move that around or to have to take over your couch long term."

He looked like he wanted to argue, but he didn't bother. "I can't believe they're kicking you out. Actually, I *can* believe it, but I hate it. And I hate that he lied to you."

"He didn't necessarily lie."

"A lie of omission is still a lie." He shook his head, his voice breathy. "He needed you to get his inheritance."

"His part in the company," I corrected, though it didn't really matter. "And Eric swears that wasn't why he was marrying me."

He didn't bother to respond.

"Oh, there's something else."

"Yeah?" He quirked a dark brow.

"Yeah. Apparently the girl he dated before me was Miles's little sister."

The curiosity was wiped from his face, replaced quickly with shock.

"And she died."

"*What?*"

"I had no idea until yesterday. I saw a picture of them together at his parents' house."

I decided to leave out the rest—Miles's accusations and their parents' wealth and connections with Phil's family. It wasn't my story to share, and Miles and James already had a contentious relationship.

"That's terrible." He was breathless, shaking his head.

I nodded. After a beat, I turned to look at him. "So, are we going to talk about the elephant in the...er, car?"

He eyed me as we came to a stop at a stoplight. "What would that be?"

"Amber. What happened Sunday night. All of it."

"Okay. What do you want to talk about?"

"Have you heard from her?"

He scratched the back of his neck. "Er, yeah. She stayed with me last night."

"She did?" I couldn't tell if the shock was more powerful than the anger I felt. The betrayal. He'd taken her side in one of our fights—something he'd never done before.

"Don't be mad. She had nowhere else to go. Once you're not so mad at her, you'll be glad I didn't make her stay in some creepy motel."

"Was that the only option?" I asked halfheartedly.

"Come on, I know she drives you crazy, but—"

"But what? Why are you suddenly Team Amber, James?"

"I'm *not* Team Amber." His voice was firm, but his eyes betrayed him. Was he actually developing feelings for her?

"That kiss told a different story."

When he looked at me, there was something oddly curious being said in his gaze. "It was a stupid dare, Colbie. You're the one who said that."

"I know, but you didn't have to do it."

"Yeah, I kind of did. And anyway, wait a second. Are you...*jealous?*"

"I'm not jealous." I folded my arms over my chest, sliding down in my seat. "If it had been anyone else, I wouldn't have cared. But it's Amber."

"And?"

"*And* she's my sister. And she's a mess. And...you know all our history."

"So, that's the only reason you care. Because it's her. Not because it's me."

I was silent, unsure if he was asking a question or what I should say in reply. Finally, he leaned forward, turning the radio up and effectively ending the conversation.

Probably better that way anyway.

WE SPENT the entire afternoon volunteering at the local animal shelter, like we did every Tuesday, though this was the first spent in painful silence. James would hardly look at me, let alone talk to me. It wasn't until we'd left and were pulling back into my driveway that he finally spoke. As he eased the car to a stop, he blurted the words out in a way that told me he'd been building them up in his head forever. "How do you feel about me, Colbie?"

"I... What?" I knew what he was asking, but I needed to stall long enough to get my head together.

"*How. Do you. Feel about me?*" He wasn't looking at me. My guess was he couldn't.

"You're my best friend. I love you. You know that."

"Yeah, but which one is it... Are you my best friend

or...do you love me?" When he finally met my eyes, the vulnerability there broke my heart.

I opened my mouth, my head tilted to the side. I needed him to understand. "James..."

He twisted his neck, looking away. "Okay. That's all I needed to know."

"You're my best friend. The closest thing I've ever had to a brother, and—"

"But I stopped looking at you like a sister a long time ago." There was pain in his words—in his voice—that shattered the resolve I had left. Pain only I could take away, but to do so would be a lie. "Do you ever think about me, at least? Do you think about us?"

I dropped my mouth open again, searching for words that would make this better. "I won't lie to you and say I've never thought about it, but it's not something I think about anymore."

"So, I missed my chance."

"We were always better as friends, James."

"How can you know that if you don't give us a chance?"

"Because I see how you look at me. It wouldn't be fair to you to give you false hope. I'm in such a weird place right now and...I need you. But I need us to still be *us*. The *us* we've always been."

His grip twisted on the steering wheel. "Okay."

"Please don't be mad—"

He held up a hand. "I'm not mad. I'm the furthest thing from mad. I understand, but I should go."

"You don't have to—"

"No, I do." He didn't need to elaborate. I could see how hard he was trying to hold it together. "But, Colbie?"

"Yeah?" I'd reached for the door handle, but dropped my hand back to my lap. Waiting.

"Don't blame me for choosing someone else, when you won't even make me an option."

I dropped my head, hearing the truth in his words. He was right. If he couldn't be mine, I had to let him be someone else's. I thought I knew who that someone else would be.

"Are we okay?"

"We will be," he promised, reaching across and squeezing my hand briefly. It was a small gesture. Just enough to let me know I hadn't ruined everything. Not completely, anyway. "But I should go."

I stepped from the car, an overwhelming sense of loss filling me as I walked toward the house.

This loss was different—it was one I'd chosen. One I could take away in a second if I wanted to.

But I needed it.

He needed it.

I had to set him free.

CHAPTER TWENTY-TWO

I stared out the window at the dark SUV as it slowed in front of my house for the fourth time that evening, squeezing my hands into tight fists. My heart was in my throat, a thin sheen of sweat on my brow.

It was the same SUV I'd noticed on the street last night, but that didn't mean anything, did it?

I was being dramatic.

Paranoid.

No one was following me.

No one was out to get me.

When I spied the second set of headlights pulling down my road, my breathing slowed just as the silver Mercedes came into view. I'd sent Eric a text to thank him for fixing my tire while I was out, but he'd given no indication he'd be over this evening, and I was feeling like too much of a bother to ask.

Already, I'd taken up so much of his time.

But I couldn't deny the relief I felt at seeing him step from his car.

Then, instead of heading for the door, he moved toward the SUV.

What?

He crossed the street quickly, and as he approached, the driver's side window eased down.

Did he know the driver? It was too dark for me to see his face. Or hers. What was he doing?

Maybe he was just checking in with him, to see if everything was okay.

Maybe he was trying to protect me.

Maybe he was just as worried after my flat tire last ni—

I froze as Eric pulled a wad of cash from his pocket, counting out several bills. He checked over his shoulder. They couldn't see me from where I stood, in the shadows of my home, watching.

He passed the cash to the driver and stepped back, patting the door.

Within seconds, the SUV began to pull away.

Then, Eric turned for the house and I had mere seconds to act. I tried to calm my nerves, to convince myself there had to be an explanation as I shot across the house, into the living room, and sank into the couch, hoping to hide the fact that I'd seen the interaction.

Where was my phone?

Who could I call?

I spotted my phone on the sofa table across the room when I heard the door open. My heart sank.

My muscles went rigid as I sat there.

Helpless.

Listening.

"You home?"

Breathe.

"In here."

Eric appeared in the doorway, a new bag of fast food in his hand. He must've stopped off at the car on his way inside. "Have you eaten?"

I glanced at the clock on the wall, then the bag of food, trying to avoid meeting his eyes. "Not yet. I wasn't expecting you tonight."

"Is it okay that I'm here?"

"If you have food, the answer will always be yes." My voice was soft, unconvincing.

"Are you okay?" He could read me like a book.

"I'm...just a little shaken up."

"What happened?" He dropped the bag and moved to my side in an instant.

"I think someone's following me." I watched his expression change from worried to confused. "Maybe the same person who hurt Phil."

"What are you talking about?"

"There's a black SUV that keeps driving through the neighborhood. They were outside last night when I got the flat tire and they were back again tonight."

His shoulders tensed. "Could it just be a neighbor?"

"Maybe, but..." I sucked in a breath, hoping this was the right plan. "I'm going to call the police and report it."

"What? Why?"

"Because what if I'm in danger? From whatever Phil *couldn't protect me from?*"

He shook his head. "*I* will protect you, okay? There's no SUV out there, Blondie. Why didn't you call and tell me? I would've come over sooner." He reached for my hands, calming the trembling I'd failed to hide.

"I didn't want to bother you." I swallowed.

"You are never a bother." He popped my bottom lip with his finger, turning his attention to our food. "Are you hungry?"

I looked down, steadying my breath. "So, there wasn't an SUV here when you got here?"

His gaze shifted back to meet mine and he stood. "Come see for yourself. No one's there."

"That's not what I asked."

When he turned to look at me again, there was a confirmation in his eyes.

"I saw you."

He shook his head. "I don't know—"

"I saw you talking to whoever was in that SUV, Eric. Why are you lying to me? Who was it?" I stood up then, sudden anger filling me. There was nothing dangerous in his eyes, only defeat.

His shoulders slumped. "I'm sorry. I didn't want to lie to you, but I also didn't want to worry you."

"Meaning?"

"The driver was hired by the Tanners to scare you."

"Scare me? What? Why?"

"I guess they think you have dirt on Phil. That you're

planning to try and ruin his reputation... Or more importantly, theirs."

"Why would I do that? I loved him."

"You know how they are. Love doesn't matter to them. Doesn't exist, as far as they are concerned. There is only power. You threatened their power by coming to the house that day. By challenging the world they've built. I never should've let you—"

"*Let* me?" I demanded. "You didn't let me do anything—"

"I didn't mean it like that. I just... Look, it doesn't matter. It's handled. You're safe. I promise you."

"How can you promise that? What did you do?"

He shifted in place, shoving his hands into his pockets. "I just talked to him. I didn't know he was the one who slashed your tire. In all the commotion, I didn't even notice him. I saw the SUV out there this morning, and I saw it again when I made it back and it clicked for me. I recognized Rodney. He's worked for them for a long time, but he's not a bad dude. I thought I could reason with him."

"And did you?"

"I got him to back off, yeah. As long as you don't cause the Tanners more trouble, I think he'll stay away."

I studied him. "Is that all?"

"That's all."

No. He was still lying to me. "Then why did you pay him?"

His head fell forward. "To protect you from what he was there for. He didn't want to do it. Like I said, he's not a bad guy, but he had a job to do. I offered to pay him whatever he wanted if he'd just *tell* the Tanners that he'd confronted you. Scared you. That you wouldn't be causing any more trouble. Without actually having to do anything."

My breath caught in my throat, chills lining the back of my neck. "Why would you do that?"

"It was the only way they'd leave you alone."

I swallowed, bitterness rising in my throat.

"Look, if you don't believe me, that's fine. But, if you call the police, it'll get back to the Tanners. And then he'll be back. You're safer if you let this go."

The weight of what he was saying pounded in my temples. "Let what go? Let…let all of it go? The truth about what happened to Phil? Everything Miles told us about Paige?"

He didn't answer.

"I can't do that."

"Blondie, you have to."

"*I can't!*"

"What are you going to do? You have nothing. Nothing on any of them. No evidence. No proof. If you cause trouble with the Tanners, I don't think I can protect you."

"That's not true!" I shouted, grabbing my laptop. "I don't just have *nothing*. I know they're powerful. I do. But I can't let this go. What if he's innocent after all? What if someone truly hurt him, Eric? What if someone killed him? He wouldn't have given up on me."

His head fell forward again, chin resting on his chest

KIERSTEN MODGLIN

as I opened my laptop and pulled up the document I'd been working on. "Here, look at this."

He leaned forward, squinting as he tried to read what I was working on. "What is this?"

"A list."

"Of?"

"Evidence."

His eyes narrowed. "Evidence?"

I squared my shoulders to him. "I know you disagree, but I'm going to the police tomorrow. I'm going to take them the letter and everything I have, everything I've learned. I want it written down so I don't forget anything. I would appreciate it if you'd come with me to back me up."

He was reading my screen, not entirely listening anymore. Finally, he looked up at me in disbelief. "Have you not been listening to a word I said? All of this proves nothing. What do you think will happen when you turn this in?"

"I don't know, but I have to do something. I'm hitting dead end after dead end. And now, I'm in danger too. You said so yourself."

"Which is exactly why you should just leave it alone, Blondie. He wouldn't have wanted this. He wouldn't have wanted you to put yourself in danger for him."

"We have no idea what he would've wanted because he's dead!" I shouted the words at him, though they were clouded with sobs. He took a step toward me, but I stepped back. I didn't want comfort. I wanted justice. I wanted to feel like I was doing something—anything—

rather than failing him. I dried my tears as quickly as they fell. "At this point, if I go to the police, at least I'm trying to get justice *if* something did happen. The Tanners should want that too. We're on the same team here, even if they can't see that. And, if there's nothing to find, then I'll know I've done what I can and I can finally try to move on with a clear conscience."

Something in his gaze shifted. "Wait, you feel guilty? Why? You didn't do anything wrong."

"I waited a year to open a letter that could've made all the difference."

"He should've been honest with you before."

"He should've. About a lot of things, but if he was involved in something—if he was in danger, or worse, if what Miles said is true—"

"What? That he killed her? Paige?"

I nodded. "I feel guilty even saying that. Even considering it. I don't want to believe it."

"I know." He glanced down.

"I know how conflicted you probably feel about this. He was your best friend and—"

"We have to protect the innocent party here." He nodded. "If that's Phil, great. But if he did something to her, her family deserves to have peace."

I was shocked to hear him agree. "So, you'll help me?"

His smile was sad. "I'll always help you, Blondie. Even if my attempts are misguided."

I placed the laptop down and stepped forward, hugging him. "Thank you. I know you don't understand, and that you're worried, but...it's important to me."

"I get it. Really, I do. I just worry about you." He tucked a stray curl behind my ear. "Have you told anyone else your plan? James or Miles?"

I shook my head. "Not yet."

"Just me?" He quirked a brow.

"Just you." I stifled a yawn, pulling back from him.

He chuckled. "I can take a hint if you want me to leave."

I knocked his shoulder with mine. "It wasn't a hint. I'm just tired. I didn't sleep well last night, and today's been...stressful. I'm sorry I accused you of...well, whatever I accused you of."

"Was that what that was?" He chuckled.

"I was just scared."

"I should probably say something about how you don't have to be scared while I'm here, but...if I'm being honest, I'm scared too." He stared ahead thoughtfully.

"We're in this together."

"Always have been."

"So, can you think of anything else to add to the list?"

I moved back to the couch, lifting the laptop again, while he stood, almost in a trance. I read over my list—trying to recall everything I already knew and everything I'd learned recently: about Paige, about the maybe-drugs in his system and the shattered champagne bottle, and the family connections between Phil and Miles. About the letter, and the woman James had accused him of being seen with just before the wedding.

As I read, Eric turned to walk out of the room without answering me.

"Eric? Where are you going?"

"To get us drinks. Be right back." He made his way into the kitchen and I dug into the bag of food, taking out two containers of pasta.

"This looks great."

He didn't answer, though I listened to the sounds of him working in the kitchen. A few minutes later, my mind back on making my list as detailed as it could be, the kettle screamed from the kitchen.

"Are you making tea?"

I placed my laptop on the coffee table, crossing the house to find him pouring hot water into two mugs. When he spied me, he held one out. "Yeah, I was going to suggest alcohol, but it seems like we could both use the rest tonight."

I opened a cabinet, pulling out a box of my favorite Sleepytime tea and dropping a tea bag into each mug. I held on to my string to dunk the tea bag a few times as I watched him do the same.

"Are you staying over again?"

His eyes widened, as if he'd forgotten I was standing there.

"Not that you have to, I just—"

"Probably not." He cleared his throat, lifting his mug to his lips to blow. "I have an early morning."

"Right. Okay."

Hearing the disappointment in my words seemed to bring him back to the present. Back to me. "But I can hang out until you fall asleep, if you want."

"Do you think the man in the SUV will come back?"

"Not tonight. Not at all if you let this go."

"I just can't."

"It's not just reckless to go against the Tanners, Blondie. It's dangerous. You understand that, right?"

I took my first sip of tea, wishing for peace it didn't quite bring me, and nodded. "I do."

The words I never got to say to Phil.

He studied me for a while and I knew there was so much he wanted to say, but for whatever reason, he couldn't. Wouldn't. Maybe he'd decided it wasn't worth the argument.

After a few silent moments, we returned to the living room and settled in for the evening, taking opposite ends of the couch while we ate our pasta and drank our tea. I finished my list and he turned on the news, though it didn't seem like he was really watching it. He was lost in his own head.

Still, it all felt oddly domestic.

Peaceful.

Safe.

Before I knew it, my eyes were too heavy to keep open. My head fell to the side, sleep overtaking me.

Just before I drifted off, someone slid the laptop from my legs.

CHAPTER TWENTY-THREE

When I awoke, it felt as if days had passed, rather than hours. It was still dark outside, the house eerily quiet. I sat up from the couch, rubbing my eyes, and tried to focus on the sound I was hearing.

A voice.

Someone was talking from another room.

More than one someone.

Their voices were low. I couldn't make out what they were saying.

I stood from the couch, wobbly on my feet, my legs still waking up, and moved toward the sounds of their hushed tones.

"You're being ridiculous."

"What choice do we have?"

It was James and Eric.

"Literally any other one."

Miles too.

"If she finds out the truth—"

What truth? I wondered.

"No. We all agreed. We stick to the plan."

"Yeah, but things are different now," Eric argued.

"For you." Miles again.

"And for her. She's planning to go to the police."

"What are you suggesting? We hold her prisoner here? Tie her up? Gag her? Maybe we should just off her right now."

My blood ran cold.

No.

I took a quick step backward, slamming into the end table. The lamp crashed to the floor and their voices fell silent.

No.

No.

No.

I thought quickly, but not quickly enough as James, Eric, and Miles appeared in the doorway. They stared at me with wild eyes.

"Please tell me it isn't true." I reached for the shattered base of the lamp on the floor.

"Careful, you'll cut yourself. Here, I can get it." Eric stepped toward me.

I shot back, holding the lamp between us as a weapon.

"What are you doing?" He tilted his head to the side.

"I heard you," I cried. "I heard what you said."

"Which parts?" Miles took a half step toward me.

I patted my pocket for my phone, spying it on the coffee table. Eric saw the move.

"Blondie, come on..."

"You don't have to do this," I sobbed.

The men exchanged glances, but it was Eric who spoke first. "Do what?"

"I heard you. About gagging me and holding me prisoner. *Offing* me. I trusted you. I trusted all of you with... with everything." I met James's eyes, my hand shaking so hard I could barely keep the lamp up. "How could you do this to me? All of you?"

"Whoa, you've got this all wrong." Eric's hands were up in surrender. "Why don't you put that down and we'll explain everything."

"Eric," James pleaded.

"This is a fucked-up plan," Miles agreed.

"Wouldn't be our first," Eric shot back.

I kept the lamp held up, backing up toward the couch ever so slowly. "What is there to explain?"

"I was joking when I said that. Blondie, you know I'd never hurt you."

"I don't know anything," I spat.

When Eric stepped closer to me, I moved back again. He reached for me, and I swung the lamp, connecting with the flesh of his palm. He jerked his hand back, blood seeping out of the wound I'd made, as he inhaled sharply through his teeth.

"Stay back!" Something in my gut had chilled. Frozen over.

The hairs on the back of my neck alerted me to danger.

"We can't let you go to the police, Colbie." James

shook his head, locking eyes with me, something in them pleading. "Not until you understand what happened."

"What are you talking about?" I shot glances between them all, trying desperately to understand.

"Please, just hear us out. We aren't going to hurt you." Something in his expression softened. "We'd *never* hurt you. You know that, right?" Eric clasped his wounded fist to his chest, the other hand still raised in surrender.

"If you want me to listen, start talking." I took another step back, eyeing the phone.

Miles darted out, startling me. I stumbled backward, expecting him to lunge for me, but instead, he snatched the phone off the table.

He huffed a breath. "Like James said, we can't let you call the police."

"What then? You're going to kill me?"

"No," came the three solemn responses.

"We will let you go to the police if that's what you want. But I need you to hear me first." Eric took another step forward.

"Hear you what? *No one's saying anything!*" I glanced around the room, checking for better weapons, or a way out. As I stepped toward the door, they moved closer. I could stop one of them, maybe, but they were bigger and stronger, and they had me outnumbered. To try to run now was a foolish plan.

My body waged war against my mind, every part of my body ready to flee—begging to flee—while my mind said it was ridiculous. That I should trust them.

Was trust what had cost Phil everything?

Or had I blindly trusted Phil and somehow lost everything?

"You don't know everything about that night." Eric held his hands up, trying to keep me calm. "We want to tell you."

"What night?"

"The night Phil died."

I swallowed, suddenly light-headed, and reached for something—anything—around me. My back hit the wall, grounding me firmly in reality. "Go on."

"Do you want to sit? I promise I won't come near you. We'll stay back. But it's a long story and—"

"*Start talking*, Eric." My arm burned from the weight of the lamp, but I didn't dare drop it. "What in the world is going on?"

He was silent for a long beat, the tension in the room filling my brain with unimaginable things. Finally, he said, "We know what happened to Phil. What really happened."

"We? *All* of you?"

"It's complicated." That was James, who was currently doing his best not to look at me.

"Will someone please—"

"*I was late that day...*" Eric interrupted me. "Do you remember?"

"Y-yes." I blinked rapidly, thinking back.

"I was late because Phil called me and asked me to make a trip to pick up a package."

"What kind of package?" I was scared to know.

"It was drugs..." Eric released a sigh through his nose, his gaze falling to the floor.

My muscles tensed. "So, you lied to me. He *was* on drugs."

"No, they..." He shook his head, squeezing his eyes shut. "They weren't meant for him."

"Then how did they end up in his system? Who were they for?" Why was I having to drag this out of them? Were they being intentionally cruel?

"He said it was for his uncles, in case they started some shit."

"What kind of drugs were they?"

"I didn't ask." Eric shook his head. "I mean, I'm not exactly a saint here either. I was in no place to judge if he needed a pick-me-up or something to calm his nerves. I thought the *uncles* thing was just an excuse."

I sucked in a breath, waiting for him to go on. How was it possible there was still even more I didn't know about the man I'd meant to marry?

"That's why he wasn't worried about why Eric was late," James filled in. "Because he knew where he was and couldn't tell you—or anyone else for that matter."

"Right. And...when I got there, he pulled me aside to tell me the truth. He'd seen Miles's name on some of Dilma's paperwork even before you were introduced to him later that day. He knew the band's name—I'm guessing you both did—but he didn't know the members. When Phil saw his name, he panicked. He was worried Miles was going to try to stop the wedding or tell you about Paige."

"What did he think you were going to tell me?" I shot a glance at Miles, who was locked on me with a dark glare.

"The truth. As I knew it, anyway. The fact that he was an ass to a family who just wanted answers only he could give. The fact that he was the last person to see her alive. The fact that he was acting suspicious, at the very least."

Eric dropped his head. "He admitted to me that something happened. Something bad."

"What? With Paige?"

He gave a sharp jerk of his head. "Yeah. He kept saying it was an accident. There'd been a fight."

Miles's hands closed into fists, and I blinked back tears as the realization of what was being told to me became clear.

"He... You're saying he actually did it? He actually killed her?" I covered my mouth, looking away.

No.

It can't be true.

It isn't true.

"Yes. Blondie, listen, the drugs were for Miles. To shut him up while Phil quote, unquote, *figured out what to do with him.*" Eric wasn't looking at me anymore, but I hardly noticed. I could see the truth of what he was saying in his eyes. Hear it in his voice.

They weren't lying. I knew it in my bones.

The lamp slipped from my hands, but none of the men moved. I gripped the wall behind me, dropping down as I felt my knees begin to buckle.

Figured out what to do with him? Who the hell was this man?

"Why didn't you go to the police?" I asked, flicking a gaze up to him. "Or tell someone? Anyone?" I forced myself to breathe, my vision beginning to blur.

He gave a sharp jerk of his head. "It wouldn't have mattered."

"Meaning what?" I choked back sobs, clutching both hands to my chest.

"Meaning the Tanners had already cleaned up his mess. And there was nothing left to find." That answer came from Miles, his voice deep and gravelly. I spied the redness in his eyes, the tears.

"Then why would they have her picture in their house?"

"To keep up pretenses." Eric ran his hands over the back of his neck, lacing his fingers together there and puffing a breath of air toward the ceiling. "Do they really look like the type to have any pictures of his girlfriends on their walls? But they aren't stupid. Keeping that picture makes them look like they aren't heartless assholes."

"Okay, but even if you couldn't—or wouldn't—go to the police, why wouldn't you at least tell me?" I demanded, folding my hands together in front of my nose, as if I was praying. Praying for this to have all been a nightmare. The kind that only comes out when you sleep. Praying I'd wake up from this. "I know you were his friend, but I thought you were mine too. I deserved to know."

"I wanted to tell you." Eric dropped to his knees in

front of me, so he could look me directly in the eyes. "Believe me, it's all I wanted to do. He was my best friend. I was processing, but I would've told you. He swore to me he was going to do it himself, though. I told him if he didn't, I would, and he swore he would. I wanted to give him a chance to be the man I thought he was." He looked away again, cheeks flaming red. "But then, James overheard."

I looked up at James, whose cheeks were sunken in as he chewed his bottom lip anxiously. No, *angrily*. He stared straight across the room at the wall, unmoving.

Pulling my attention back to him, Eric went on. "He was going to tell you. He wouldn't let you marry him without knowing the truth. But...Phil wasn't having it."

My blood chilled. "What did he do?"

Eric's eyes shifted. "Phil threw him on the ground when he wasn't expecting it. Tried to hold him down. James fought back. Held his own." He said it with the cadence of a proud father. "I tried to break it up, but we were making a lot of noise, and then Phil grabbed a bottle of champagne. He smashed it on the table and he...he held it up over James. He wasn't going to let him leave to tell you."

"Wha..." I covered my mouth, willing James to look at me from where he sat, but he wasn't. How was any of this real? It sounded like a movie, not something that could actually happen to anyone I knew.

"I wasn't thinking. I just acted... James had the syringes and insulin in the wine fridge, so I pulled them out. The drugs were meant to be ingested, but there was no way I was getting him to ingest anything, so I had to try something. I filled it up and shoved it into his hip and, before he even realized what I'd done, he was out cold."

My head tugged back in shock. James moved his hand to his neck, as if remembering that moment.

"You *drugged* him?" I shook my head, feeling dizzy.

"I didn't have a choice!" he insisted, his eyes bulging. "I needed to come up with something, and I had to do it fast."

"He saved my life," James said, finally meeting my eyes from where he stood. "Plain and simple. Only one of us was walking out of that room. Phil made that clear."

I rubbed a hand over my eyes, so unbelievably overwhelmed.

"So, then we... We talked about our options." Eric licked his lips, breathless. "We could've called the police or told you... But it was our word against his. Phil was a lawyer. From a respectable family. We were nobodies. I was just his alcoholic friend and James has no connections either."

"And when I told you about seeing Phil with that woman, you didn't believe me. How was I supposed to think you'd believe me then?" James's words cut deep.

He was right.

I was blind when it came to Phil. I never questioned him. Never doubted his intentions. He made me believe my own best friend had lied to me... But now... Now, I was certain James had been telling the truth. All Phil had ever told me were lies.

I had no idea who he was.

"I found Dilma, asked her if she could buy us some extra time. I told her Phil had a bit too much to drink and wasn't feeling well, so we just needed to sober him up. She agreed to stall for as long as she could."

"That was why the ceremony was delayed..." It began to all click into place for me.

"But then, Miles came back." Eric's gaze fell to him across the room. "He got tired of waiting to talk. When Dilma told them there was a delay, he thought Phil was going to try to bail. He barged into the room without warning and found us instead. James was roughed up, the champagne bottle was shattered, and Phil was passed out. We tried to make up some excuse, to tell him he was drunk, but...it didn't take long for him to figure us out. We were still too emotional. Too panicked."

"So...all three of you knew about this. All this time?" Betrayal stung at my core. How had they let me cry myself to sleep over a man who was a monster? Didn't a single one of them think I deserved the truth?

"We couldn't tell you, Blondie. We were protecting you, too. We didn't want you to have to carry that burden. Our burden." Eric's hands landed on my knees.

"But...I don't understand. You just knocked him out, right? Did the drugs you gave him cause his heart to stop?"

"Not exactly..." He held my eyes, tilting his head to the side slowly. "We... It was my idea. Don't blame them. I knew what Phil was capable of. I saw him for what he was in that moment, and the reality of so many other moments came to me then—moments when he'd yelled at a waitress over something stupid or...or gripped your wrist a little too tight when he was angry. I cared about you, Blondie. Too much to let you marry him. To put you at risk."

"Me too." James squared his shoulders to me. "I told you I promised your mom I'd take care of you. I did what I had to do. *We* did."

"What about you?" I looked at Miles. "You didn't even know me. I was a stranger. Why would you help them?"

"You were a victim in his mess. Just like Paige. If we took care of him, we'd never know the truth about what happened to her. I knew that. I weighed the reality of it in that room, with the clock ticking." He stood too, moving to stand next to James, his arms folded. "But if we didn't do it, and if we couldn't prove what he'd done, that meant he'd marry you and you'd be in danger. And not just you. How many other women would there be? How many other women would he hurt?"

The air was sucked from my lungs as the truth swam through me, rising and falling as real as the vomit in the back of my throat. Would Phil have ever hurt me?

Like he hurt her?

Had he hurt others?

"At the end of the day, as much as I loved Paige, as much as it will always haunt me to never get the truth, you were still here. Still alive. I had to protect you because I couldn't protect her."

Tears pooled in my eyes, spilling over onto my cheeks as I fought to catch my breath.

"We agreed. We'd be willing to do whatever it took to protect you. Go to jail, if that's what it meant. Or worse." Eric's hands gripped my knees again, reminding me they were still there.

I swallowed down the bitterness in my mouth. "*No…*" I couldn't find the words.

"Miles distracted the crowd. Played music, got them dancing. Did what he could to keep them away from where we were. And James… James left and went back to his office to clean up. And to get what we needed in order to finish what we had to."

My breath caught in my chest.

"He didn't feel anything," James offered, his voice low. "It was just like falling asleep."

The words washed over me. They were the same ones he'd said once when he'd had to put down a sick dog at the shelter.

I clasped my hands together, pulling away from Eric. My elbows dug into my thighs, my face buried in my forearms as sobs tore through me.

I'd wanted the truth, and now I had it. But just like Eric warned, I didn't like it. Didn't want it. It was too much.

Too much to handle.

Too much to survive.

"You actually did it? You killed him?" I silently pleaded with James to tell me it was a lie.

"He didn't." Eric called my attention back to him. "I did."

"*No.*" Somehow, that was worse.

He spoke over my sobs, just needing to get the words out. "So neither of us could blame the other. He brought the medicine and showed me where to put it so no one would find the injection site. But I did it. So, if you're going to hate anyone, if you're going to turn anyone in..." His eyes held pure terror, but his voice was steady. "Hate me, Blondie. If that's what you need, blame me. This is all on me."

I squeezed my eyes shut, my chest constricting with heavy sobs.

"And, for the record, we'd do it again."

I looked up to James, shocked by his words. "*What?* How can you—"

"We would. The guy deserved it, Colbie. More than that, he didn't deserve to be with you. And, if this was the only way to keep you safe, I'd do it a million times over."

"Me too." Eric's voice was softer, riddled with pain.

"Me too." Miles gave a stern nod.

"But, James, you could've lost your practice. Your license. You guys could've gone to jail. You could've been *killed*." I was overwhelmed by all the potential and very real consequences. "This was so stupid of you. So, so stupid." I dropped my head, a grim thought slamming into me. "Eric, he was... My god, he was your best friend. Your brother. How could you..." I touched his chest, thinking of all the times the three of us had spent together.

I thought of all the times Eric had cried on my shoulder after Phil's death. Thought of the very real grief he suffered over his loss. A loss he purposefully decided he could handle, if it meant protecting me.

"We were careful. The drug we gave him occurs naturally in the body. It wouldn't look suspicious on his autopsy." James's answer was cold. Matter of fact.

"And none of that matters anyway. We didn't care, Colbie. Don't you get that? We love you. We wanted to protect you." Eric grabbed my hands, pulling them to him.

Suddenly, something clicked for me. "That's why you've all been around so much this year. You were..."

They exchanged a look.

"We wanted to make sure you were okay. Even knowing we did what we did to protect you, we also knew that we were going to be breaking your heart. We knew what you'd already lost, and we knew what this would do to you. We knew it would break your heart in ways we couldn't begin to understand. So, we've been here for you in every way that we can this year. We can't replace him. We know that. And we can't ask you to forgive us." Eric's voice quivered. "But your hatred—your unwillingness to forgive us—is another consequence we're willing to bear if we have to."

"I..." I sniffled, trying to think. Trying to breathe. I just wanted it all to stop. "I don't know what to think. What to say." The three men dropped their heads. "But I do know that you all have been the best friends—the family—I've needed this year. I know that what you did was out of love, even if it hurts, even if it scares me, and I know that I don't know what I'd do without any of you."

The truth came pouring out of me. "Over the past few days, I've learned I didn't know Phil all that well after all. And I still love him. That doesn't go away. But...I also understand that he was dangerous. I do. And I understand why you did what you did, even if I wish you didn't have to."

Eric dropped his head. "We've wanted to tell you. Every time you cry for him... Knowing I did that, I brought you this pain. Blondie, you have no idea how badly it's killed me."

I pulled him into a hug then, both of us broken beyond repair, but willing to try anyway.

"We wanted to protect you," James said. "From him, but also from the truth."

"But now the Tanners think you know what he did to Paige. And, if you go to the police, I don't know that we'll be able to protect you from them, no matter how hard we'll try. I couldn't let you risk all of that without telling you the truth." Eric pulled back, rubbing his eyes. "He's not worth your life."

"No, he's not. *You* saved my life. All of you." My gaze danced between James and Miles. "And I didn't even know about it." I shook my head. "I see that as clearly as I see everything you've done for me this past year."

"But when I saw that letter—" Eric's gaze was haunted. "The guilt was eating at him, even though he never let on. Maybe he was going to turn himself in after all. Maybe he was going to tell Miles the truth or go to the police..."

It was true.

Everything he was saying.

Based on Phil's letter to me, he was planning to tell me the truth. He was going to come clean after the wedding.

What would I have done? Would I have let him reason with me? Let him explain it away?

Would I have had to carry that burden for the rest of my life, like I'd now have to carry this one?

"We can't know." I looked away, clearing my throat. "We'll never know. All we have is our truth. What we know. Where we go from here."

"So, where do we go?" James asked. "What do you want to do?"

Miles stepped forward, sliding my phone onto the coffee table.

I eyed it, a raw sort of pain swelling in my gut. I shook my head, unable to think past the moment I was in, and turned my attention away from the phone and back to them. "I won't turn you in, if that's what you mean. As much as you love me, I love you all the same." I offered them the most reassuring smile I could muster, though I knew it was a terrible attempt.

My promise seemed to relieve some of the tension from the room. I laid my head back against the wall, closing my eyes.

Over time, James and Miles came to rest on the floor next to us. For a long time, none of us said anything. We just breathed. Just existed.

Just felt.

That was life, wasn't it?

Messy.

Painful.

Terrible.

Beautiful.

And everything in between.

So, we sat. Our makeshift family in the in-between. And we felt it all, all that had been and all that would come.

Whatever it would be, I had to believe we could face it together.

CHAPTER TWENTY-FOUR

E very breath was painful now. Raw. Terrifying. I thought about that as we sat in silence throughout the night, each of us dozing off occasionally, but no one sleeping soundly.

Maybe that was their punishment. And mine too, now that some of the guilt was mine to bear.

If I wanted to, I could turn them in. Bring the bad guys to justice, so to speak. But I wasn't completely sure there were any clear-cut bad guys in the story.

Not really.

And if someone disagreed with me? If they were actually named the villains by some sort of villain-deciding council?

I wouldn't turn them in anyway.

I meant what I told them. I loved this group. My boys. Dysfunctional as we were, we were a family. And families, I'd learned at a very young age, were not something you took for granted.

How had they managed it for so long, though?

Just living and breathing with this secret crushing the air from their lungs? Would it always be this painful? This raw? This terrible?

I wasn't sure.

And I wasn't sure I wanted it not to be. If I went numb to this, somehow it might be worse. If feeling it all was my punishment, if I had to live the rest of my life with a crushing pain in my chest whenever I thought of my best friends and my first love, then so be it.

Miles was first to leave.

"I could never thank you enough, you know that, right? The others, they had their reasons for helping me, but you were a stranger."

He tapped my chin with his thumb. "Paige would've liked you. You...remind me a lot of her. Always have."

I looked down. "Hey, you never told me why you were looking at Phil's social media. The night we played Truth or Dare."

He shrugged one shoulder. "I wanted to see how you used to look at him."

I lifted a brow.

"To see if you looked at James the same way." He shook his head. "I want you to find happiness again, Colb, okay? It matters to me."

I smiled through my tears. "Someday."

With a distant hug, he promised to be back soon, though I thought it might be a few days.

I'd wait as long as it took. He deserved time.

The sacrifice he'd made for me was a big one. The biggest. For a stranger. And the thing holding him close to me this year had been his guilt.

I wanted him to be free of that.

When James approached me next, I rested my head on his shoulder. "I love you, you know that?"

He rubbed my back. "I do."

"I want to say I can't believe you did this for me, but that would be a lie. I can because all you've ever done is what's best for me." I squeezed him tighter and he squeezed me back, saying everything we couldn't put into words in our embrace.

When we broke apart, we both had tears in our eyes. I cleared my throat. "Hey, can I ask you something?"

"Yeah. Anything." His response was instant and sincere. When he met my eyes, I saw fear in them. The same fear I'd seen for so long but now understood.

I glanced toward the doorway to the kitchen, making sure Eric was still in there making coffee, giving us freedom to talk.

My brows pinched together as I stared at him. "You know, for the longest time, I couldn't figure it out."

"Figure what out?"

"I couldn't figure out why your letter bothered me so badly. From the wedding box. I thought it was because it was so short, when I'd expected more, but that wasn't it. That wasn't why."

He shifted uncomfortably.

"It hit me last night. Thinking over the wedding, I

remembered something I hadn't before. I remembered seeing you writing your letter to me. It was when I left the room where I'd been waiting with Jerry for the ceremony to start, just before we found Phil. You were in the hallway while I talked to Annie. I could see you, off in the distance. By the box." I narrowed my gaze at him, my next words pointed. "You were writing for a really long time."

He checked over his shoulder, his mouth opening as if he were going to say something, then closing again.

"It was you, wasn't it? The handwriting didn't match Phil's, but I thought he was nervous, or writing on his lap or something. But it was you... You wrote his letter."

He rubbed his lips together, a confirmation in his silence.

"Why? Why would you do that?"

"It was what he owed you. What he should've been man enough to say. Man enough to do. And, if he couldn't, someone should've. I wanted you to get closure. To get peace."

I thought back, recalling the parts of the letter that had always stood out to me.

It was selfish of me to love you, Colbie. Selfish of me to marry you...

I hope I'm still with you by the time you open this letter. I hope that you know the truth about me—who I am and what I've done. And I hope that, by some miracle, I'm still right by your side...

Know how badly I wanted to protect you from all of this.

"Part of it was from you... Wanting to protect me... Wanting me to know who you were... Calling Phil selfish for marrying me."

He tipped his head forward. "I was caught up in the moment. Parts were what I wanted to say to him. Parts were what I wished he would've said to you. Some..." His gaze was slow to meet mine. "Some of it was me talking to you. Saying what I'd never been able to say."

"James..."

"It's okay." He shook his head, and for the first time, I thought he might actually mean it. "You deserve someone who loves you, Colbie. But more than that, you deserve someone you love back. That letter was my way of trying to repair what I'd played a part in breaking. But we're good." He rubbed a hand over the back of his neck. "Honestly. I needed to hear the truth from you. I think I've been waiting all my life to hear it." His smile was soft. Sad. "I freed you a year ago. Thank you for freeing me now."

Tears blurred my vision. "I wish I felt differently."

"No, you don't." He smashed his lips to one side, giving a slow shake of his head. "And I know someone else who doesn't either."

I studied him, trying to decipher what he was saying.

"If it can't be me, it should be someone who loves you just as much as I do." He jutted his head toward the kitchen, where I suspected Eric was waiting to say goodbye to me alone. "That man gave up everything for you—including his best friend—and he would do it again in a heartbeat. I don't know that I could ever love someone enough to give you up for them. So, if you feel the same way, I hope you'll tell him." He leaned forward, pressing his lips to my cheek, and I closed my eyes, feeling all of what he was saying. "Life's too short, you know?"

And I did.

I wrapped my best friend in a hug, the silence filled with all the things I still wanted to say but couldn't. Somehow, I knew he understood anyway.

He always had.

When he pulled away, Eric was standing there.

Something on his face told me he'd overheard at least part of the conversation. The important part.

James slipped out the door, leaving us alone, and I swallowed.

"You heard that?"

His gaze swept over my face slowly, his head rising with a gentle nod.

"Was he wrong?"

He swallowed hard. "No. He wasn't wrong." A small smile played on his lips. "And he said it better than I ever could've."

"You love me?"

He looked down, my heart thudding in my chest so loudly I wondered if he could hear it. When he looked back up, there was a seriousness in his features that I'd never seen. "Of course I love you, Blondie. God, maybe I always have. I've never really been good with words when it comes to you. And I was terrified to say or do the wrong thing, so I just...didn't. But it doesn't matter how I feel about you, because I won't let myself lose you if you don't feel the same. So, what matters is how you feel... about me." He hesitated, scarlet splotches creeping up his neck. "How do you feel about me?"

I blinked, the answer on the tip of my tongue before I had to contemplate it. "You were always there. Always. When I needed you, without saying a word, you've made this year bearable for me. So many nights, I've fallen asleep crying in your arms. You offered me a place to stay. You've taken care of me, and I thought it was just because of him..." Tears stung my eyes and I looked away. How had I not seen it before? Why hadn't I realized?

"Maybe it was, at first. Or, maybe I thought it was. But that changed somewhere down the line. You were always the girl just a little out of reach. But then, you weren't. And that terrified me. *Terrifies* me."

I moved toward him without even realizing my feet were moving, and in seconds, his hands were on my hips as they had been so many times before but, at the same time, nothing like they'd ever been before. "Ask me again."

"I don't want to push you. Last night was a lot."

I nodded, tilting my chin toward his ever so slightly. "It was."

"You're still grieving and... I can be whatever you need for as long as you need."

"You already are." And it was true. Terrible. Painful. True. "Ask me again, Eric."

He sighed as he spoke. "How do you feel about me, Blondie?"

I ran a finger across the stubble on his cheek, a pulling sensation sweeping through my core. "I love you. In a way that's different than how I love James or Miles. I know it without having to think. Without having to question myself. You make me feel seen and understood in a way no one ever has. I'm sorry I didn't see it before."

I felt the breath he released somewhere deep inside of me. He'd been waiting to hear those words. It was written all over his face.

"If you don't stop me, I might kiss you." His voice was so low, I wasn't sure I'd heard him, but I didn't need to. He could say it all without saying a word.

With his gaze bouncing from my eyes to my mouth and back again, he moved forward, inch by inch, nearly in slow motion. His breath hit my lips first, and mine parted involuntarily.

As his eyes finally closed, he pressed our lips together with caution. We sank into it, our kiss a sigh of relief after a year of so much unspoken.

Life was too short to leave anything unspoken for a moment longer. To leave anything left unsaid.

His hand slipped up my back, gripping the back of my head, and he said everything he needed to say without uttering a single word.

In his arms, I felt safer than I had in an entire year.

Safe, but scared.

Shattered, but whole.

Overwhelmed, but peaceful.

I felt everything with him.

All and nothing and everything in between.

Phil had given just as much as he'd taken from me, and someday, I'd learn to cope with that. For now, things were beautifully broken, just as they should be.

ENJOYED IF YOU'RE READING THIS...?

If you enjoyed this story, please consider leaving me a quick review. It doesn't have to be long—just a few words will do. Who knows? Your review might be the thing that encourages a future reader to take a chance on my work!
To leave a review, please visit:
https://mybook.to/ifyourereadingthis

Let everyone know how much you loved
If You're Reading This... on Goodreads:
https://bit.ly/3dfWrVT

STAY UP TO DATE ON EVERYTHING KMOD!

Thank you so much for reading this story. I'd love to invite you to sign up for my mailing list and text alerts so we can be sure you don't miss my next release.

Sign up for my mailing list here:
kierstenmodglinauthor.com/nlsignup

Sign up for my text alerts here:
kierstenmodglinauthor.com/textalerts

ACKNOWLEDGMENTS

First and foremost, to my family, Michael and CB—thank you for all that you do for me every single day. Thank you for making this life so exciting, for believing in me with your whole hearts, and for being behind me every step of the way. I couldn't do it without you. I love you both.

To my bestie, Emerald O'Brien—thank you for your encouragement, for being my sounding board, and for being the first in line to tell me I can handle whatever comes my way. Love you, friend.

To my immensely talented editor, Sarah West—thank you for always believing in the story, no matter what shape it comes to you in. Thank you for trusting my voice, my ambitions for each story, and my (sometimes) untrustworthy characters. I'm so grateful for you.

To the proofreading team at My Brother's Editor—thank you for your eagle eyes, for catching all the stubborn typos, and for not complaining when I need you to explain the difference between lie and lay over and over (and over) again. I couldn't do this without you guys!

To my loyal readers (AKA the #KMod Squad)—thank you for believing in me. For cheering me on, for trusting me with each new story, for rooting for my characters (even the questionable ones), for loving my twists, for all of the reviews, the purchases, the gifted copies to friends and family, the recommendations, the emails, the messages, the tags, the Insta stories, TikToks, blog posts, and everything else. Growing up, I wished for you, but I never could've imagined how genuinely blessed I would be with the greatest readers in the world. Thank you for giving me the most beautiful life. I'm forever grateful for each and every one of you.

To my book club/gang/besties—Sara, both Erins, June, Heather, Dee, and Rhonda—*you guys!* What would I do without you? Seriously, my Wednesday nights would be so boring. I'm incredibly thankful that our book club has become so much more than a book club. Your friendships mean so much to me. I don't know how I would've made it through this past year without all the laughs and love. You're officially stuck with me.

To Brittany Cormier—thank you for the initial spark that inspired this story. I love when ordinary things turn into the best plot ideas. Thank you for trusting that I could turn something so innocent into something totally sinister.

Last but certainly not least, to you—thank you for supporting my dream by taking a chance on this story. It means the world to me. I truly hope you enjoyed Colbie's story as much as I loved telling it. Whether this is your first KMod novel or your 34th, I hope it was everything you could've hoped for and nothing like you expected.

ABOUT THE AUTHOR

KIERSTEN MODGLIN is an Amazon Top 10 bestselling author of psychological thrillers and a member of International Thriller Writers, Novelists, Inc., and the Alliance of Independent Authors. Kiersten is a KDP Select All-Star and a recipient of *ThrillerFix*'s Best Psychological Thriller Award, *Suspense Magazine*'s Best Book of 2021 Award, a 2022 Silver Falchion for Best Suspense, and a 2022 Silver Falchion for Best Overall Book of 2021. She grew up in rural western Kentucky and later relocated to Nashville, Tennessee, where she now lives with her husband, daughter, and their two Boston terriers: Cedric and Georgie. Kiersten's work is currently being translated into multiple languages and readers across the world refer to her as 'The Queen of Twists.' A Netflix addict, Shonda Rhimes superfan, psychology fanatic, and *indoor* enthusiast, Kiersten enjoys rainy days spent with her nose in a book.

Sign up for Kiersten's newsletter here:
kierstenmodglinauthor.com/nlsignup

Sign up for text alerts from Kiersten here:
kierstenmodglinauthor.com/textalerts

kierstenmodglinauthor.com
www.facebook.com/kierstenmodglinauthor
www.facebook.com/groups/kmodsquad
www.twitter.com/kmodglinauthor
www.instagram.com/kierstenmodglinauthor
www.tiktok.com/@kierstenmodglinauthor
www.goodreads.com/kierstenmodglinauthor
www.bookbub.com/authors/kiersten-modglin
www.amazon.com/author/kierstenmodglin

ALSO BY KIERSTEN MODGLIN

STANDALONE NOVELS

Becoming Mrs. Abbott

The List

The Missing Piece

Playing Jenna

The Beginning After

The Better Choice

The Good Neighbors

The Lucky Ones

I Said Yes

The Mother-in-Law

The Dream Job

The Liar's Wife

My Husband's Secret

The Perfect Getaway

The Roommate

The Missing

Just Married

Our Little Secret

Widow Falls

Missing Daughter

The Reunion

Tell Me the Truth

The Dinner Guests

ARRANGEMENT TRILOGY

The Arrangement (Book 1)

The Amendment (Book 2)

The Atonement (Book 3)

THE MESSES SERIES

The Cleaner (The Messes, #1)

The Healer (The Messes, #2)

The Liar (The Messes, #3)

The Prisoner (The Messes, #4)

NOVELLAS

The Long Route: A Lover's Landing Novella

The Stranger in the Woods: A Crimson Falls Novella

THE LOCKE INDUSTRIES SERIES

The Nanny's Secret

Made in the USA
Columbia, SC
09 September 2022